SEVEN O'CLOCK TARGET

SEVEN O'CLOCK TARGET

JOANNE PENCE

QUAIL HILL PUBLISHING

Quail Hill Publishing

PO Box 64

Eagle, ID 83616

Visit our website at www.quailhillpublishing.net

First Quail Hill Publishing E-book: July 2019

First Quail Hill Print Book: July 2019

SEVEN O'CLOCK TARGET

1

The decaying inner-city street was deserted except for two children. And him.

He stood in the shadows of a gutted, vacant building and watched them.

A little girl wearing blue denim overalls and a pink T-shirt followed her brother. He walked fast, the way older brothers often did, and the girl had to run to keep up. Her curly brown hair, pulled back into a ponytail, bounced and swung with each step.

The boy wore a San Francisco Giants baseball cap. He wasn't much taller than his sister, but stockier. His hair was a lighter shade of brown and cut short.

The sun was setting and the evening fog had already rolled in off the bay making the dank, dingy area gray and forbidding.

Those kids shouldn't be alone in this neighborhood, he thought, and especially not on this street. It was dangerous. The buildings, mostly warehouses and factories, had closed years earlier and were either empty or taken over by squatters. Used syringes, condoms, shell casings, and worse littered the nearby grounds.

If you were my children, I wouldn't let you play out here.

The two stopped and stared at the smallest building on the block. One story tall, its ugly, ash-colored outer walls looked like painted cement. The sign over the front entry—VENTURA BROS MORTUARY—had weathered so badly it was hard to read.

He wondered if those kids had any idea what a mortuary was. If so, they'd run from it. He had worked there one summer when he was young, and it still gave him nightmares.

But instead of running, the little boy studied the low, flat structure with curiosity. He turned onto what was once a driveway along the side of the building. It led to the back lot where, when the business was live so to speak, the bodies had been delivered. Now, the driveway was nothing but chipped and broken asphalt with weeds sprouting up through the cracks. At the back of the building, near the empty lot, was a metal door and beside it a wood-framed window. The bars that once protected the window from intruders were now on the ground, rusted and propped up against the wall.

He crept nearer the children. He especially enjoyed looking at the pretty little girl. Her cheeks were apple-red and her large blue eyes showed spunk and character as she glared at her brother.

"I don't like it here," the little girl firmly stated.

With good reason.

"Molly, look. This window isn't locked." The boy ignored her complaint as he pushed on the double-hung window. It slid upward a fraction of an inch, just far enough for his small fingers to get under the opening and lift.

"I said I don't like this," Molly insisted, louder. "I want to go home."

"Not me," big brother announced. "I want to see what's inside."

"It's almost seven o'clock. Daddy told us to be home by seven. Besides, I'm hungry!"

"So?" The boy, trying to sound tough, wrinkled his mouth in disgust at his sister's lamentations. "Anyway, it's not a mortuary anymore."

"I don't know what that is, and I don't care. Let's go, Porter!" Molly folded her arms. Her scowl was even fiercer than her brother's had been.

As the man watched her, he couldn't help but chuckle. He had to smile at the way even young girls could pout, whine, and get their way around their brothers. Around all men, if his experience was at all usual.

The boy pushed the window up as high as he could and boosted himself onto the windowsill. "You wait here, and I'll tell you all about it … maybe." Porter tumbled inside.

The girl stood on tiptoes peering in.

Such fun! He covered his mouth to stop his soft chortles from bursting into a boisterous guffaw. He remembered times like that with his own sister, times so long ago. She was the only person he allowed himself to remember, the only person he missed. He never knew his father and tried his best not to remember his mother. And he certainly didn't miss her.

"What if somebody catches you?" Molly cried.

Framed by the window, Porter looked out at her and grinned. "Who would do that? Nobody lives here. You're such a scaredy-cat." Then the boy disappeared from sight.

He wondered what the boy was up to and grew increasingly frustrated until he heard the youthful voice cry out, "Whoa! Awesome!"

His breath caught. What, he wondered, had the boy found?

"I want to see." Molly tried to boost herself onto the sill the way Porter had done, but couldn't. The boy reappeared, grabbed her arm, and pulled her into the building.

When the children didn't come out again, he followed. It was easy for him. He had a key to the side door.

He entered a small back office. His eyes went to the desk that the mortuary's last boss, a mean son-of-a-gun, had used. The fat, bald ogre would sit there, large hands with pudgy, hairy fingers folded over a protruding stomach as he bellowed orders to his intimidated workers all day long. It heartened him to see the desk now covered with dust, as were the office's three gray file cabinets, a table, and an old black rotary phone.

He peered into the hallway.

He didn't see the children.

Damn!

He hurried down the hallway, over a yellowed, linoleum-covered floor, and past doors labeled "Men" and "Women" to the foyer at the front of the building.

To one side of the foyer was the mortuary's main entrance, and across from it was what had once been its largest viewing room.

The doors to the viewing room were open, and he heard the low murmur of voices. Childlike voices.

He peeked inside.

Old, half-rotted drapery hung beside the windows and along the back walls, while thin sheets had been pinned up to cover tall windows. Some sheets had fallen, allowing a few beams of sunlight to stream in, just enough to show that the green paint on the walls had become streaked and faded, and that the dark hardwood floor was scuffed, scratched, and littered with rat droppings.

Only a few wooden chairs remained in the room, facing a far wall that had been set up to look like a stage.

"This place is creepy," Molly murmured.

Yes, little girl. You don't know the half of it.

If he were a nicer guy, he would scare them, make them run away and never come back. But he wasn't all that nice.

"This is where they put dead people in coffins so their friends can come and see them." Porter did his best to appear smart and worldly.

"After they're *dead?*" Molly sounded horrified.

"That's what I've heard."

The two walked up to the front "stage" and noticed a cut-out area on the floor. The boy knelt down to inspect it. "I wonder what this is. It looks like a trapdoor." He tried to find a spot where he could take hold of it and lift it open, but was having no luck.

The man smirked. He knew what the cut-out was. He doubted any mortuary used such a thing these days. But many decades ago, when this place was first built, it was considered quite a practical innovation.

He saw Molly eyeing the nearby wall. It had two large buttons. *No!* He wanted to scream, to stop her. But he kept watching.

She pushed the upper button, and nothing happened. But then she pushed the lower one, and the platform Porter was studying made a whirring sound. The boy eased back.

"What's it doing?" Molly stepped to Porter's side, and both stared, amazed, as the platform descended to the basement.

"Maybe you'd better bring it back up." Porter's voice lost it toughness and now sounded a little scared and nervous.

That's right, kids! You don't want to have anything to do with what's down there.

Molly ran to the wall panel and pushed the upper button. The platform slowly rose up and settled back in place.

"Wow!" Porter shouted. Then, in a fit of daring, he jumped onto the middle of the platform. "Push the button again."

Molly did, and Porter rode down to the dark basement. "Hey, I see buttons here just like the ones by you." He pushed the upper button and jumped on the platform as it climbed.

"I want to ride, too," Molly announced when Porter reached her once more. Hitting the down button she jumped onto the platform next to Porter. Both children laughed, a strange mixture of delight and fright as the platform descended with them on it.

He crept toward the opening. He had been in that basement many times, but he'd always taken the stairs.

Down there the mortuary owners not only stored unused coffins but also those that held the dead after being embalmed, awaiting the trip upward to the viewing room.

"What is this place?" Molly's scared voice wafted up to him.

He could imagine how scary she must find the basement. It had no windows and the light switch was on the far end of the room, at both the top and bottom of the staircase leading up to the main floor. For the children, the only light came from the platform opening, a light that now grew fainter as dusk deepened. He bent low so he could see and hear them better.

The hollow sound of their footsteps echoed on the cement floor as they walked away from the platform. The footsteps matched the sudden pounding of his heart as a startling realization struck him.

"Look at those big boxes." Molly's voice was tiny, fearful.

"Coffins," Porter said. "I wonder if they put the bodies in coffins down here and then use that platform to get them upstairs where people could see them."

Exactly! His heartbeat drummed so loudly in his ears his whole body trembled. Even so, he was impressed that Porter could work out the reason for the platform. It saved the morticians and their staff from having to carry heavy coffins up the stairs.

"What if they have people inside them?" Molly's voice was little more than a whisper.

"Don't be silly. Nobody leaves bodies lying around," the boy announced. "Besides, they stink after a while."

"*Eeuwww.* But who would be here to smell them?" she asked.

"You're just being a dumb girl."

He heard the girl cry out, "Porter! Look! What... who... are *they?*"

"Oh, child," he whispered, his shoulders sagging from the weight of his decision. "You shouldn't be so nosy." And with that, he pushed the up button, and the platform rose.

2

At seven o'clock Monday morning, San Francisco Homicide Inspector Rebecca Mayfield was already at her desk on the fourth floor of the Hall of Justice building in San Francisco's South of Market district. She hadn't been able to sleep and decided to get a head start on the problem that was bugging her. More than bugging her. It was disrupting her life; even preventing her from attempting any plans for the future.

Someone had targeted her. Not necessarily to kill her—although more than once, that could have been the result. But, she believed, to cause her to leave her job. And she was sick of being anyone's prey.

Her face was pinched from weariness and her pale blond hair pulled back into a barrette at the nape. She wore little makeup, and her blue eyes had a tinge of red she hoped Visine and black coffee would help fade. Her clothes reflected her personality, practical and logical—black slacks, a crisp white blouse, and a black woolen jacket now hanging on a nearby coat rack.

As she waited for her computer to go through its log-in and security routines, her expression was dark, hooded, and almost as grim as the homicide bureau itself. Soot-covered windows along the back wall and burned-out bulbs in several of the light fixtures lent a solemn air to the open room filled with gray and green metal government issue furniture—desks, file cabinets and book-shelves—along with a water-cooler and the world's oldest still-functioning percolator-style coffee urn.

Recently, several of her cases had overlapped in a way that presented her with a picture of corruption emanating from City Hall. All fingers pointed at some person or persons in City Hall having directed a real estate scheme that laundered money. The scheme had ended, many of the bankers involved were now serving time, but Rebecca hadn't yet been able to determine which government officials were involved.

The problem was for a cop, any cop, to get past the wall of protection that both politicians and bureaucrats always erected around themselves. But she wasn't about to give up.

Her problem was that, as long as she was being targeted because of her investigations, she refused to do anything that might cause others to be in jeopardy because of her.

Specifically, Richie Amalfi, the man she had somehow, crazily, fallen in love with, had asked her to move in with him. As much as she would have liked to, there was no way in hell she would move into the home while someone was trying to kill her! If she did, and anything happened to him, she didn't know how she could bear it. It was best to live as she always had since her early twenties—alone. Except for Spike, of course, her little dog, a strange looking but lovable mixture of a hairless Chinese crested and a Chihuahua.

She believed the key to figuring out who was behind the attacks on her could be found in the death of the mayor's former chief-of-staff, Sean Hinkle. A couple of other homicide inspectors had investigated the suspicious death, but after finding a suicide note—plus receiving more than a little pressure from Homicide's chief to get the story off the front page of the *San Francisco*

Chronicle—the inspectors quickly and quietly determined that Hinkle had committed suicide.

Rebecca wasn't buying it. She never had, and that was the reason for her early morning appearance at work. She was determined to sift through the case and to look for any clues that might have been overlooked. But she couldn't let anyone know she was doing an unauthorized review of a closed case. That type of "initiative" top brass frowned on. Especially when it involved the city's mayor, deputy mayor, and those close to them. That the deputy mayor had direct supervisory responsibility over the police commissioner only made the situation more complicated.

That morning, Rebecca had no sooner looked up the case number of the Hinkle files when her phone buzzed. It was the dispatcher.

So much for looking into Sean Hinkle's death that day. A homicide had just been reported.

Richie Amalfi awoke to an empty bed.

He sat up and ran long fingers through wavy black hair, trying to get it to fall at least somewhat in place. He knew a night of tossing and turning played havoc with it, and with a small spot at the crown that had thinned as he approached age forty, he needed to take good care of every strand he had.

But hair problems were the last thing on his mind right now. Rebecca was. As usual.

A part of him wished he could end this off-again, on-again craziness of their relationship. He hated it, and she did, too. A part of him even wished he could walk out of her life and not look back. But he'd tried that.

And failed.

Like some idiot, or *stunad,* as it mother, Carmela, would say, he had asked her to move in with him. He'd never done that with any other woman.

Rebecca had refused his offer.

And she wouldn't tell him why.

It was crazy. He'd never had to work so hard at getting a woman to want to be with him. He was used to the women he was seeing wanting their relationship to move along much faster than he did. More than once he had to all but batten down his doors and windows to keep them away.

Even his mother had tried to push him into a marriage with the daughter of one of her Italian friends. Talk about a vision of hell!

Ironically, of all the women he'd dated, the one he fell the hardest for Carmela didn't much like. Maybe it was because she and Rebecca were both strong, both used to getting their way, and neither took guff from anyone. If he was smart, he'd have nothing to do with either of them.

He guessed he wasn't smart because he loved them both.

He put on his robe and headed out to the kitchen to make his morning Americano. As he crossed the living room, the scent of flowers hit him. He glared at the pale pink peonies in a silver vase. They all but turned his stomach. Even worse was the small colorful bouquet of mixed flowers on the kitchen table.

He'd bought them for Rebecca, knowing she loved fresh flowers. Not only had they not helped to convince her to move in with him, they hadn't even convinced her to stay with him last night!

As he pushed buttons on his automatic espresso machine, he thought about Rebecca. He should have known flowers wouldn't make a difference. She wasn't like any woman he'd ever dated.

None of them had been dedicated cops who'd gotten on the wrong side of "the elite" in the city. Rebecca had overturned some big rocks in City Hall, and what she found wasn't pretty.

And the people who'd been hiding under those rocks didn't

like being exposed. Richie, frankly, didn't care at all about big city government corruption. As far as he was concerned, it was a fact of life—as common as birds and bees. Or more fitting, vultures and hornets.

But now, the bastards were interfering with his happiness.

It was time to act.

3

R ebecca saw black-and-white police cars and paramedic vans filling the street as she approached a small house in the city's Bayview-Hunters Point district.

It was one of the few areas in San Francisco where gentrification and resulting high prices hadn't yet hit. Driving to the crime scene, she had passed an abandoned housing project, several decrepit factories, and some oddities such as a defunct mortuary.

Neglect was the word for what had happened here. Neglect of buildings and the people who lived in them.

She parked as close as she could get to the crime scene. Around her, police radios crackled and a few older people stood just beyond them to watch the action.

The house itself needed paint, and a short chain-link fence enclosed a front yard with dead, matted grass where a lawn ought to have been. Not even weeds grew here, Rebecca thought, as she put on a crime-scene protecting jumpsuit and booties.

"I'm Officer Cortez." The young policeman who had been the first to arrive on the scene met her and introduced himself.

"What have we got?" she asked.

"The victim's name is Daryl Hawley. He rents this house. He

and his wife recently separated. She showed up this morning to pick up their kids and found the body."

Rebecca nodded her thanks and followed Cortez into the house. The small living room had a sofa, a chair, and a TV. A stout woman huddled on the sofa. She held several pieces of Kleenex to her nose and mouth. Her full cheeks were tear-stained, her bushy blond hair so dry it seemed it would snap off if brushed too vigorously. She wore a dark green dress and black leggings.

"That's the victim's wife," Cortez said. "Tracy Hawley."

Rebecca wondered where the kids were now, and guessed someone, a relative or police officer, might be keeping them away from the crime scene.

She continued through the living room to the small kitchen. To one side of the room was a table covered with used bowls and plates, and on the other, beneath a window, a pile of dirty pots and dishes all but buried the sink. And in the center, Dr. Evelyn Ramirez, the city's medical examiner, bent over a man's body. He lay sprawled face down on the floor. A sea of blood surrounded him from a bullet wound to the back of the head.

Dr. Ramirez glanced over her shoulder at Rebecca, then stood upright and stretched her lower back. "I'm getting too old for this job. Particularly this early on a Monday morning."

Sure, Rebecca thought. Even early in the morning, the ME appeared meticulously put together, flawlessly made-up, and her hair perfectly styled. "That's not age," she said with a wry smile. "It's your wild weekends."

Evelyn snorted. "Not this weekend, believe me."

The two had become friends over the years, and despite Rebecca's curiosity, this wasn't the time or place to pursue this conversation. Instead, she swerved to the situation at hand. "Does that gaping hole in the back of the victim's head tell me what I need to know?"

"Cause of death. Right." Evelyn pulled off her rubber gloves.

"Of course, I'll autopsy him to see if there are any surprises. I will say, judging from the powder burns, the gun was held at a very close range."

"Time of death?" Rebecca asked.

"It's been a while. I'd say last evening, probably seven o'clock give or take thirty, forty minutes on each side."

Rebecca nodded, then faced Cortez. "You mentioned kids earlier. Where are they now?"

"Good question," Cortez replied. "They have two kids, boy and girl. The husband had them this weekend, but when the wife showed up to take them to school, she found him dead. She doesn't know where the kids are."

That sounded bad. A quick glance at Cortez told her he was thinking the same thing.

"What's being done about finding them?" she asked.

"Patrol is out canvassing the area, and officers are checking with the neighbors."

But if the father was killed last evening, Rebecca thought, where have the kids been all this time? Her skin prickled at the thought.

Just then her partner, Bill Sutter, arrived. He was usually the last to show up at a crime scene. Sometimes Rebecca wondered why she put up with him and didn't go to her boss and demand a new partner—one who worked with her as a team, not someone only half-interested in their casework because he was too busy thinking about retiring from the force.

She filled Sutter in as they went through the Hawley home working their way around the technicians dusting for fingerprints.

They saw no immediate evidence of a break-in. In fact, the location of the wound, the way the gun had been held near the victim, even the way the victim fell, were typical of a contract execution.

Rebecca found a phone buried under the newspaper on the

kitchen table and bagged it as evidence. From his wallet and papers she learned he had a steady albeit low-paying job as a driver for RX Wholesale.

In the bedroom was an old laptop. A quick search of the area around the laptop turned up a small spiral notebook with passwords. "Thank you, Daryl Hawley," Rebecca whispered. She arranged for them to be delivered to her desk in Homicide.

Finally, it was time to talk to the ex-wife.

The woman stiffened, squeezing the wad of Kleenex she'd been holding as Rebecca and Sutter approached. Then she dropped it on the coffee table and rubbed her hands against the skirt of her dress. Her eyebrows were thinly penciled and her eyelids so puffy from crying that her eyes were practically hidden. Fear filled her face as she stood. "Where are my kids?" she demanded, her voice high and trembling.

"Police officers are out looking for them," Rebecca said calmly. "They're talking to your neighbors. Can you think of anywhere they might have gone?"

"No. Their friends don't live around here." She all but spat out the words and seemed more angry than anything. It was obvious to Rebecca that her tears were about her kids and not her dead husband. "They don't know anyone here except Daryl."

"Is their school nearby?"

"No. Even when we lived here, I took them to a private school in the Sunset district. We now live close to the school."

Her words surprised Rebecca. This hardly looked like the home of a couple who could afford a private school. "Might the children have called someone to pick them up?" Rebecca asked. The Sunset district was on the other side of the city.

Tracy Hawley's hands clenched as she all but shouted, "They don't have phones. They're just little kids." But then her face crumpled and her tears fell again. "My God!"

"I'm sure they're all right. They're probably scared and

hiding," Sutter said, his voice surprisingly soft and comforting. "We'll find them for you."

"I hope," she whispered and grabbed the Kleenex again to wipe her eyes.

Rebecca gave her a moment, then asked, "What's your full name?"

"Tracy Jane Hawley." She threw in her address and date of birth, making Rebecca wonder if she'd had previous encounters with the police.

"Am I correct that you and Daryl Hawley are separated?" Rebecca asked.

"I moved out two weeks ago. I was thinking about filing for a divorce."

"Why did you leave?"

"It's not important now," she whispered.

Rebecca knew the answer to that question could be quite important, but she let it rest a moment. "What brought you here today?" she asked.

Tracy's voice turned flat. "I came to pick up the kids and take them to school. I can't depend on Daryl doing it." She squeezed her eyes shut and turned her head as if trying to dispel the vision.

"Was the front door locked when you got here?" Rebecca asked.

She thought a moment, and then her shoulders sagged. "No, I guess it wasn't. I rang the bell. I wasn't expecting Daryl to answer, but I thought my kids would. When they didn't, I tried the door. It opened." Her breath caught. "Unless the kids were playing outside, we kept the door locked. Often with a dead bolt."

"Then what happened?"

"I came inside and found Daryl." She sounded defeated.

"Did you touch anything?"

"No. I was sure he was dead by the way his eyes stared, cold and blank. I called nine-one-one, then ran outside to look for

Molly and Porter. I went up and down the street yelling their names, but didn't see them. A few neighbors came out, but they were no help. Then, the ambulance arrived, and soon after the police." Again her tears flowed, and her voice grew loud, desperate. "They stopped me from trying to find my kids and made me sit here. *Where are they?*"

"Do you have a picture of them?" Rebecca asked.

Her hands shook as she grabbed her tote bag and dug through it, finally coming up with a wallet bulging with credit cards. She looked through it, then shook her head. "All these are too old. Oh, wait."

She easily found her cell phone. Practiced fingers flew over it. "Here. Molly is six and Porter eight."

Rebecca took the phone and looked at two cute, brown-haired, blue-eyed children smiling at the camera.

"I'll need a copy of this," Rebecca said, and at Tracy's nod, sent one to her email address.

"Why is all this happening?" Tracy whispered.

"We'll find them, Mrs. Hawley," Rebecca said. "Like my partner said, they're probably scared and hiding somewhere."

Tracy nodded, but didn't look convinced.

"Could you tell me," Rebecca asked, "where were you last evening? Did you see your husband or children at all yesterday?"

Tracy sniffled and shook her head. "No. I... I met someone at work. We spent the day together, then went to dinner. I got home around ten and went to bed. Alone. I guess we didn't hit it off as well as I thought we would."

"Where do you work?"

"Blaxor Pharmaceuticals."

"How long have the two of you dated?"

"That was our first date."

"And what's his name?" Rebecca asked.

Tracy's eyes widened. "Why all these questions? You can't think that I ..."

"We have to check everyone and everything," Rebecca said. "I'm sorry."

While Tracy turned to her phone to get the contact information for her date, Rebecca wondered if Tracy knew what the time of Daryl's death had been. At that time, on a Sunday evening, it was likely the kids were in the house when their father was killed. If so, they were witnesses.

Rebecca had tried to sound upbeat, but her guts warned her things might not work out well at all.

Henry Ian Tate III, called Shay, sat in the study of his home in the exclusive Presidio Heights area of San Francisco. He was alone and listening as the front door was pulled shut. A chill rippled through him.

Shay was a mystery to everyone who knew him. That would have included friends if he had any. He might have patrician good looks, light blond hair, pale blue eyes, and a propensity for expensive clothing that included ascots and silk-blend sports coats, but his stern expression was both off-putting and intimidating to most people.

He had many acquaintances—most of whom hadn't wanted to encounter him to begin with and definitely wanted no repeat confrontations. And he had a couple of people that, these days, he routinely worked with, Richie Amalfi and Vito Grazioso. Other than them, his dealings with people were limited to his housekeeper and his daughter.

Whenever asked what his job was, he'd reply, "Contractor," and then give the cold, flat stare that caused men not to question him further.

When Richie needed help, either technological or strong-arm, he would go to Shay. Shay was always ready to help. Or, he used to be.

Lately, he'd been questioning that part of life. No, that wasn't true. He'd begun to question every part of his life.

Nine years ago, he met a Lebanese woman, Salma Najjar, in San Francisco. Despite Salma being already married—an arranged marriage—they fell in love. Although Shay had tried over the years to forget her, he never really had. Recently, they met again, and that was when he had not only learned that he had fathered a child, Hannah, but also that Salma could be charged—and likely convicted—of murder.

Shay believed she had killed at least one person, and possibly two. He knew there was a current moratorium on capital punishment in California, but the state could reinstate the death penalty at any time. Two murders could make that a possible sentence.

He couldn't say whether the murders were justified or not. That wasn't his call to make. But he completely understood Salma's motives and had vowed to do all he could to protect her.

He was also convinced that Salma had no choice but to run. Taking Hannah with her would have been all but impossible, and no life for the girl. Also, Salma didn't know how her Lebanese husband, Gebran Najjar, would treat Hannah once he learned she was the product of his wife's illicit affair.

For all those reasons, Salma had all but begged Shay to take Hannah and to raise her himself. Shay also helped Salma escape the law … and the country … as he took his daughter into his home.

Shay had spent little time around children. If he bothered to think about them at all, which he rarely did, it was to conclude he didn't particularly like them. For the life of him, he had no idea how he was supposed to suddenly behave like a parent toward one. And a girl, at that.

Fortunately, his live-in housekeeper, Mrs. Brannigan, had not only raised three children of her own, but had several grandchildren. To Shay, she suddenly became worth her considerable weight in gold.

She was a genuinely good and dependable person—she had to be to meet his exacting standards—and he felt quite at ease relying on her to take care of the child. In fact, for the past weeks, he had done all he could to stay out of Mrs. Brannigan's way and let her deal with Hannah's everyday needs.

Now, he rushed from the study to the living room, hurried to the window, and looked down at the street. Hannah was walking to school, Mrs. Brannigan with her. He knew he should be the one walking her, protecting her, but what did he know about talking to an eight-year-old?

He watched until he could no longer see her tiny figure in the distance. As she disappeared from sight, an eerie foreboding struck.

He quickly turned away from the window. There was no reason for him to feel such unease. People sent their children off to school every day. He shouldn't worry.

But still…

It was ironic, he thought, how he had known Hannah only a short time—hadn't raised her or even known about her—and yet she already meant everything to him. God forbid what he would do to anyone who tried to hurt her or take her away from him.

He was already working on the necessary legal issues.

Although Salma Najjar had given him notarized documents declaring Shay was Hannah's biological father and that she wanted him to have custody of the girl, California law held the legal presumption that a woman's husband was the father of her children. Therefore, Shay contacted an attorney to help him overcome that presumption.

To help satisfy the courts, he and Hannah had taken a DNA

test. Although he was awaiting its results, he had no doubt she was his daughter. A person only needed to look at them to know. Both had uniquely shaded blue eyes that darkened along the outer edges of the iris to a deep lavender. Also, the girl's long-limbed, lithe build, the way she cocked her head, even the way she spoke, were incredibly like him.

And she looked nothing like the stocky Gebran Najjar.

He had reluctantly taken care of her school needs thanks to Mrs. Brannigan who, after Hannah had been living with him for two weeks, announced, "That child needs to go to school."

"But you can teach her here at home, and so can I," Shay had insisted. "She'll do better than at any school."

"That's not the point." Mrs. Brannigan declared. In her early sixties with short gray hair, medium height, and a warm disposition, she could be every bit as forceful as her boss when necessary. "She should be with children her own age. She can't sit around here with an older woman and a father who hides in his study all day. She misses the people she once knew. She needs to make new friends."

As much as he hated to admit it, he knew she was right.

He carefully researched private schools in the area, and was pleased to find an exclusive school, The Sutcliffe Academy, only a few blocks away. He was determined Hannah would go there.

Since he was skilled at doing "specialized" internet research, he put that ability to work before going to meet the school principal. It had paid off.

As he expected, the principal initially announced that the Academy was simply too full to admit Hannah. A few words from Shay, however, about the principal's fortuitous and sudden accumulation of funds for his mortgage payments after being seriously in arrears … and the principal swiftly discovered he had room for Hannah after all. He didn't even question why she was being admitted as "Hannah Tate," when her birth certificate showed "Hannah Najjar."

At that point, the principal could scarcely stop shaking.

Now, finally, the day had come for Hannah to head off to her new school.

Shay, who had spent time in Iraq and Afghanistan, and had even done some clandestine work for the CIA, couldn't bear the idea of placing his daughter in the care of a bunch of teachers. What did teachers know about the ways of the world? About evil? Most of them were little more than kids themselves.

They hadn't seen the things he had; hadn't known how cruel people could be.

He couldn't—wouldn't—let her out of his sight.ha"She's not going," he had announced to Mrs. Brannigan that morning before breakfast.

"Yes, she is, Mr. Tate." Mrs. Brannigan gave him one of her sternest glares. She was one of the few people he knew who wasn't intimidated by him. Mostly, he respected her for that. At the moment, he hated her.

"I can't do it," he confessed, finally.

Mrs. Brannigan pursed her lips. "I'll take her today. You can do so tomorrow."

He had stayed in his study until the two left the house, and although he had watched them from the window, he was tempted to go out and follow in his car to make sure they got there safely.

Idiot! He told himself. When had he turned into such a wuss?

His phone rang. It was Richie.

4

Richie strode into the Leaning Tower Taverna on Columbus Avenue, the front panels of his sports coat flapping as he headed for his favorite booth, the one in the very back. As soon as he entered, the familiar smells of peppery red spaghetti sauce, garlic, oregano, and a hint of fennel washed over him as soothing and comforting as a warm blanket. It was truly his home-away-from-home.

He gave a nod to the waitress, and a glass of Chianti reached the table almost as quickly as he did.

Soon, Vito Grazioso and Shay, his closest friends and business associates, joined him. First things first, they got down to the business of ordering lunch. Richie, as usual, ordered carbonara, his favorite. Shay, as ever, refused to eat anything prepared in a restaurant, and ordered a cup of Earl Grey tea. And also, as always, Vito needed time to study the menu.

As much as Shay was a puzzle to Richie, Vito was as easy to read as the morning sun. Where most people saw him as two-hundred-fifty pounds of pure muscle, to Richie he was all heart. As brawny and intimating as he was to those who didn't know him, to Richie, Vito was one of the kindest and most loyal people he'd ever come across. Finally, Vito ordered a meatball sandwich and a bottle of Coors Light since his wife told him he needed to lose some weight.

At that, Richie nodded sagely and did his best not to catch Shay's eye. While waiting for the food—and tea—to arrive, Richie explained the reason for the meeting.

"I called you here because I'm sick and tired of Rebecca being in danger. I want to know who's behind the attacks on her, and to make them stop."

"I agree about the danger, boss," Vito said. "I'm glad I was there to help her out of a few jams, like the time someone tried to run her down as she crossed the street, or that time a guy rammed the back of her SUV and pulled a gun on her when she got out to survey the damage."

"You did good, Vito," Richie said, knowing how much Vito thrived on well-deserved praise.

"The worst," Shay said, "was when she was sent to a fake homicide on the beach in the middle of the night. At least two guys dressed as cops were involved, and one of them, or someone else, waited there to ambush her."

Richie shuddered. "Don't remind me. That was close for all of us."

The waitress brought out the tea and beer. Shay put a tea bag in the hot water to steep. "It also told us that whoever's behind this knows a lot about police procedure and was even able to get a beat cop's uniform."

"Which means," Richie said, "whoever is behind these attacks is most likely someone high up in city government, the police department, or both." The thought made his stomach feel sour. He knew Rebecca had been lucky so far, but how long could it last? "Rebecca is a threat to them. One way or another, they want her out of their lives."

"What do you want us to do, boss?" Vito asked.

"We'll start at the top—the mayor and his staff," Richie said. "Shay needs to look at their financials and we'll concentrate on anything odd, especially large sums going into or out of accounts. Then, Vito, you'll need to watch them, follow them to see what they might be up to. We need to find someone who's gotten in over his head financially or with women, or drugs, or whatever. Someone who'll need a special kind of service." He raised his eyebrows. "The kind of service I'm good at providing. Someone who'll think of me as his go-to guy."

"Got it, boss," Vito said.

"Once we finger a staffer who looks like a good mark," Richie said, "I'll find a way to meet him or her and offer assistance to help cover up the secrets. Just the fact that I show up and know those secrets is usually enough to rattle most people and get them to listen. Once I'm inside, I'll get a good idea of what everyone is up to. But be careful. Any leaks about what we're doing could mean disaster for Rebecca."

As soon as Rebecca let her boss, Lieutenant James Philip Eastwood, know that the two young children of the murder victim were missing, she expected the Inspections Bureau Special Victims Unit would handle that aspect of the case. It would be up to her and Sutter to concentrate on finding the murderer.

Still, to Rebecca's mind, as important as her job was, she couldn't help but think about the kids and the need to search for them. The possibility that whoever killed the father had kidnapped the children was high, and she could only hope they were still alive.

Rebecca had dealt with the murder of a teenager twice, and they were horrible, wrenching crimes for everyone involved, the police as well as parents and friends. She couldn't imagine handling a young child's murder and hoped she never would. The thought of it spurred her to ignore what Lt. Eastwood said and continue to hunt for them.

The best scenario, to her mind, was that the kids headed back to their mother's apartment and were lost and scared in the big city. If so, someone should report them soon. A bulletin with their photos had already gone out to all patrol units in the city to be on the lookout for them.

She guessed there was enough ambiguity about where they might be and whether or not they were in any immediate danger that no Amber alert had yet been issued. Sutter had promised to see to the release of pictures of the kids to the media. Surely, if the children were wandering about the city, they would be spotted.

In the meantime, she and Sutter decided to canvas the neighborhood themselves. Often, after studying a crime scene, patrol officers knocked on doors while the homicide inspectors returned to the Hall of Justice and scoured databases to learn about a murder victim's background, prior arrests, phone records, financial situation, and so on. But with missing children, time was of the essence. If a neighbor saw or heard anything that might give them a hint as to what had happened in that house the night before, and where the children might be, they wanted to hear about it as quickly as possible. Plus, in a neighborhood like this one, people tended not to talk to uniformed police. At least Rebecca and Sutter wore plain clothes.

They went first to the home east of Hawley's rental. The small lawn area was overrun with weeds and no lights shown through the windows. When no one answered their knocks, they hopped the fence to the back yard and looked through grimy windows to the home's interior. It was empty, seemingly unoccupied.

As they approached the house to the west side of Hawley's, an elderly man opened the door. He had been watching the police activity from his window. His name was Dennis Crumley, a retired widower, and he had lived in the neighborhood, in the same house, for thirty-five years.

"I didn't look out my window at all last night," he said when Rebecca introduced herself and asked if he had seen anything. "In fact, I think I fell asleep early with the TV on."

"Did you see Mr. Hawley's children?" she asked.

"I saw them, all right. A lively pair. They seemed like good kids. They played out on the street all weekend, running into and out of the house. But once it started to get late, he'd usually call them back inside. I assumed he did last night, as well."

"Did you see them or hear them this morning?" Sutter asked.

"No, can't say I did. It was all pretty quiet until Hawley's wife showed up and started running up and down the street yelling for the kids. I tried to stop her and ask her what was going on, but she wouldn't listen."

"Okay," Rebecca said. "And, can you tell me which houses are occupied on this street? Some seem to be empty."

"Yeah, lots of places need work and the owners don't want to bother." He pointed out several houses she might check.

"If you think of anything, or see anything, please call me," Rebecca said, handing him her card.

He took the card and studied it a moment. "You know, I did hear something. But I suspect it was a car backfiring. Although it might have been a gunshot."

Rebecca stepped forward. "What time?"

He shook his head. "I'm not sure. I'd say around seven o'clock, but TV is messed up on Sunday nights. If I had my regular programs, I'd know for sure."

Rebecca asked him to call if he remembered anything more, then she and Sutter headed for the four other homes on the block that Crumley said were occupied. Two had no one home, and residents in the other two hadn't seen or heard anything.

The inspectors headed for the next block to find that the neighborhood quickly turned from one with small homes to an area that had once been commercial. As Rebecca studied the large, old, mostly empty buildings, she could imagine scared kids hiding in any one of them. Still, it seemed they would have come out by now.

She and Sutter entered the buildings that weren't locked or boarded—ones young children might easily have entered—but nothing indicated the children might be there. Everywhere they went, they called the children's names, praying for a response that never came.

"We should wrap this up," Sutter said, "and head to homicide. The SVU should be here by now. No sense covering the same territory as them."

"You're right," Rebecca said. "I just want to check out one more block with homes. Why don't you go back, get started with some database searches, and I'll meet you there in an hour or so."

Sutter frowned. "It's not a great idea, you going alone to these houses and old buildings."

Rebecca patted the Beretta on her hip. "I'll be careful."

5

P orter Hawley opened his eyes and saw nothing. He took a
moment to remember...

And then it all rushed back at him.

He remembered looking around the dark, dusty basement and
seeing boxes, crates, and a staircase that went up to a door that
must have opened to the main floor. But more than anything, he
remembered a bizarre group of dolls seated on child-size tables
and chairs in what looked like a schoolroom scene. They were
near the wall opposite the staircase. They were what Molly saw
that had scared her so badly.

And, he had to admit, scared him as well.

Porter thought of how he had been staring at those strange
dolls when he realized the sound he heard was the platform being
raised. He had spun around to see it floating upward from the
basement floor.

He had run to it, already waist-high and grabbed on. He
managed to climb on. But Molly was slower, and it was already
too high for her. His gaze jumped from her up to the opening
in the ceiling. There, he saw the face of a stranger peering
down at him. A man. His heart nearly stopped. But as quickly

as their eyes met, the man pulled back, his face no longer visible.

Porter froze, unsure for a moment what to do, but quickly realized he couldn't leave Molly. And he was afraid to keep going upward. The man's expression had been fierce, ugly.

He slid off the platform, letting himself drop to the ground. His legs and ankles ached from the jolt of landing on the hard cement.

He and Molly had clutched each other's arms, crying and shaking in fear as they watched the platform settled into the floor above them.

The basement had now become pitch black. He had seen no windows, and no light shone along the edges of the platform or the door at the top of the stairs. He expected the stairs led to a door, a way out. But once the room darkened, he was too scared to move, especially when he thought of the creepy group of dolls. He felt disoriented and soon had no idea which direction led to the door or to the controls for the platform.

He and Molly had screamed for what seemed like hours for someone to let them out, to please, please come and find them. They had shed copious tears, and eventually, somehow, managed to fall asleep on the cold cement floor. He had no idea how long they slept. All he knew was now that he was awake, his legs, arms, and back were stiff and sore from lying on the hard ground, his head ached from crying, and his throat felt raw from shouting for help. Help that never came.

Plus, he was hungry. And thirsty. And scared.

Molly was still asleep when he heard footsteps.

"Wake up," he whispered and shook Molly's shoulder.

She opened her eyes to darkness. "What—"

"Listen. Someone's coming."

Molly immediately stopped speaking. Her hand grasped his.

Porter felt his heart pounding with fear but also hope as he listened to the rattle of a doorknob. "Maybe someone's found us."

Then, as the door opened at the top of a flight of stairs, daylight streamed into the basement.

He and Molly stood, squinting in the sudden brightness, ready to run up the stairs when a portly figure dressed in black filled the doorway. The figure wore a hoodie pulled forward to hide the face.

Porter froze.

The figure bent low and placed a tray on the top step. "Eat." The voice was low, hushed, and male. Then he reached back, picked up two buckets and placed them beside the tray. "And use these so you don't soil yourselves or the floor any more than you already have!"

Then the figure backed out of the doorway.

"Wait, please!" Porter shouted, running up the stairs. "Let us out of here. We want to go home."

The door slammed shut before he reached it and darkness fell over the cellar once more. The basement seemed even darker than before.

He dropped to his hands and knees and continued to the top of the stairs where he found the tray of food. He opened the bag. "It's hamburgers," he said. "And, I think, a carton of milk and what might be a bottle of water. Can you find me, Molly?"

"Yes. I'm on the stairs. I'm coming up."

She reached him quickly. The two were so hungry and thirsty they ate and drank everything that had been left for them.

It wasn't until they had finished that Molly whispered, "Do you think he'll come back?"

Porter suddenly realized they should have saved some of the food and drink. What if the man didn't return? What would they do? How would they get out of here?

"I don't know," he whispered in answer to her question. "I just don't know."

6

San Francisco City Hall is an ornate Beaux-Art neoclassical structure built to show the resilience and reemergence of the city after tremendous destruction visited on it by the 1906 earthquake and fire. The building occupies two full city blocks, capped by the tallest dome in the U.S., a full forty-two feet higher than the one in Washington D.C.

On the second floor, Deputy Mayor Dianne Cahill stood at the window looking out at Civic Center Plaza. She was an attractive woman in her early fifties. Most people in the city knew of her and knew her story. Born in San Francisco to an African-American mother and a white father who both had been radicals at U. C. Berkeley, they had raised her and her younger sister in a Marin County commune. Dianne had put herself through college and devoted herself to working for the people of San Francisco by getting into city politics. She had been a powerful political operative in the city for years. Mayors came and went, but "Madam Deputy" had ensconced herself as the true power inside city government. She knew where all the bodies were buried, and no one who crossed her could survive. Many people predicted much bigger things for her than the deputy mayor position, but she had not been interested.

Or, not until recently. Now, Mayor Cornelius Warren had his eye on the governorship and good money was being bet that this time Dianne Cahill would run for the mayor's seat. And she'd get it. Few of the city's politicians were as popular with the voters. She was competent and ran the city according to her vision for it.

At the moment she was on the telephone with the mayor's new chief of staff, Clive Hutchinson. She had phoned him.

The two of them were once an item—a secret item because he was only an analyst in the accounting division when they first met. She soon saw to it that he was promoted to head of the department, and they wanted to be sure the appointment was never viewed as anything but merit-based.

With Hutchinson's latest promotion to chief-of-staff, Cahill had hoped they could let the world know of their courtship. But recently Hutchinson had one excuse after the other to keep from seeing her. At work, he was cordial and friendly, but nothing more. When she tried to question him about his suddenly busy schedule, his excuses sounded legitimate. But she was nobody's fool and sensed exactly what was going on.

"I just heard that Daryl Hawley has been found dead," Cahill said.

"Hawley … the name is familiar," Hutchinson remarked.

She couldn't believe he didn't remember. "It should be." Her tone was terse, worried.

"Oh, God," Hutchinson murmured.

"Yes," Cahill sneered, knowing he had finally put it together. "And guess which homicide inspector has the case?"

"Mayfield?"

"That's right."

"But surely she won't—"

"Are you willing to chance it?" she asked.

Hutchinson was quiet a long moment. "I hate this, Dianne."

"So do I," she admitted quietly.

"What are you going to do about it?" he asked.

You? Why not "we?" She swallowed hard to keep the bitterness from her tone. "I've got a contingency plan going. I was hoping I didn't have to use it, but now, I've got no choice." She drew in her breath before adding, "It won't take long, but when I'm through, it'll be more than this case that Inspector Mayfield will no longer be handling."

"A contingency plan?" He sounded impressed. His voice softened as he added, "I like it."

Her heart skipped a beat as the soft tone brought back so many memories. But then she gripped the phone harder as anger warred with tender emotions. "You used to like everything I did," she said sharply. Other women might avoid being so open about their feelings. She didn't. To her, the hurt in her voice, the acridity of her words, should give him fair warning. If she could make life hell for a homicide inspector, just think what she could do to him.

She hung up the phone without saying goodbye.

At home that afternoon, Shay kept watching the clock. It was 3:30 p.m. Mrs. Brannigan should have returned home with Hannah some fifteen minutes earlier. The school was less than ten minutes away.

After what seemed like an eternity, Shay looked at the clock again. 3:40.

He should have been working on Richie's request. He had, for a while. But at three o'clock his nerves were so on edge he left his study for the living room where he watched the second hand move on the grandfather clock.

He hadn't lived the "friendliest" sort of life, and had made a lot of enemies. People who might want to get even.

People who might see him having a child he cared about as a way to do just that.

The thought made him sick with worry. And fear.

He paced. Where were they?

He had always assumed people would arrive where and when they were supposed to. If they did, all was good. If they didn't, it wasn't as if he cared.

But now, he constantly cared—and worried—about Hannah, where she might be, what might happen to her, and who was saying what to her. He told himself he shouldn't be such a Nervous Nelly. After all, for the past eight years she'd gotten along just fine without him.

Of course, she had had her mother then.

He wondered how he would ever survive her teen years.

He was ready to jump out of his skin by 3:50 when, finally, he heard the main door to the house open and shut.

Once a mansion built in the early 1900s, Shay had converted the enormous home into two small apartments on the ground floor and his large apartment on the second. On the roof was a deck with a view looking out on the area that had once been a military fort, the Presidio of San Francisco, and was now a park.

The tenants in the downstairs apartments were even quieter than Shay—the only kind of tenant he tolerated. Others, he immediately evicted. Despite rent control and a myriad of tenant rights in the city, none of them ever went to the authorities to complain about the eviction.

Now, he realized the sound of the main door might have been because one of his tenants used it. But he couldn't stop himself from leaving his apartment and hurrying to the top of the elegant, carved cherrywood staircase.

To his great relief, he saw Hannah and Mrs. Brannigan

walking up it. Instead of greeting them with joy, he thundered, "Where in the world have you been?"

"It's nothing to bother yourself about," Mrs. Brannigan stated. "Leave us be for a while. All is well, and you needn't worry."

He looked at Hannah and saw that her nose seemed a little too shiny as did her eyes. Instead of greeting him with a smile, she gave him a quick glance and then dropped her gaze to the ground.

All sorts of crazy ideas went through his head. Clearly, she had been crying. But why? Was it something he had done? Or something someone else had done to her? If anyone hurt her ...

"What's going on?"

Mrs. Brannigan ignored him as she entered the apartment, took Hannah's coat and backpack, and brought her into the kitchen where she seemed to take her time pouring the girl a glass of milk and setting out a plate of the chocolate chip cookies she'd baked that afternoon.

He hovered over them both.

"Wait," his housekeeper whispered.

But he couldn't wait. As Hannah sat at the kitchen table and took sip of milk, he sat across from her. "You look upset," he said to her. "Is something wrong?"

"As Mrs. Brannigan said, it's really nothing, Shay," Hannah announced in her odd way of speaking. Most of the time she sounded like the eight-year-old she was, but other times she came across as more adult than he was.

"Are you sure?" he asked.

She dipped a cookie into the milk and seemed focused on making sure she got just the right amount of milk on the cookie before she lifted it out again. Too much and it would turn soggy and fall apart in the glass; too little, and the cookie would remain hard in the center. "Mrs. Brannigan explained to me I was being too sensitive, and that I was letting people who had no right at all get the better of me."

It was all he could do not to smile. Her mother had told him that Hannah had gone from saying "Mama" to using long sentences in no time flat. "What do you mean, get the better of you?" he asked.

She ate the wet half of the cookie, but then her mouth tightened. "It's nothing. I've decided I really don't care about them."

"I see," he said.

She looked up at him, her small face tight and indignant as she announced, "They're just some crummy kids. And not my friends. They don't know about me and they don't matter to me." But then she put the second half of the cookie down on the napkin in front of her and stared at the glass of milk.

Shay almost reached out to touch her slight shoulder, as if that might help ease the burden she seemed to carry, but then he drew back. "Someone said something that upset you." His voice was gentle. "What did they say, Hannah? Please, tell me what's wrong."

She shrugged as if to show it didn't matter, but when she spoke her voice was hushed, and he could hear the hurt in it. "They asked me who I was. They wanted to know why I showed up in their school. They asked if I had moved here from far away, and when I told them it was none of their business, they acted like I was really weird. Then they asked about my mother and father. When I didn't answer them, they said I didn't know any of the answers. They said maybe I didn't belong in their stupid school, and that I should just go back to wherever I came from."

She bowed her head so as not to look at him.

Shay didn't know how to react. He'd seen so much really bad shit in his life, that her being questioned and even somewhat bullied by some other third-graders seemed like nothing to him. That made him immensely relieved, jump-for-joy kind of relieved … if he ever showed joy about anything.

On the other hand, this was all his fault. He had sent her to one of the best private schools in the area—the type he had gone to as a boy. He didn't want her back in public school, and definitely not back at the school she had attended before everything in her life changed. He thought he was doing a good thing, but he'd forgotten about the type of kids at an exclusive school like the one he had chosen. That type hadn't been a problem for him because he had "belonged." He had been like a lot of the kids Hannah encountered, learning from their parents to be more concerned about a person's background and "pedigree" than his character.

"I can see where that would have upset you," he murmured. "And I can understand those kids having all kinds of questions about a smart and lovely girl like you suddenly showing up in their class. They want to know where you came from and why you're there. Not that it's any of their business, of course, but kids tend to be nosy as I'm sure you know."

That brought a hint of a smile to her face. "Yes, they are." But she still didn't go back to her half-eaten cookie.

He felt he had made a little inroad and quickly continued. "I remember when new kids showed up in my classes, sometimes they weren't treated very well. Over time, things settled down. But it'll take a few days."

He saw tears well up. She took a sip of milk as she blinked them away. Finally she said, "Tomorrow I still won't have answers to their questions. And I won't the next day either. So I'm not sure what I should say or do. Maybe … maybe I should go wherever my mother is."

Her words hit like a knife to his chest. "I'm afraid you can't do that, Hannah. I can't even do it." His words were scarcely more than a whisper. "But I know that, more than anything in the world, your mother wishes she could be with you. Maybe someday you and I will find her. But not yet. Do you understand?"

Hannah just looked at him with those peculiar eyes that held so much wisdom but also youth. "I understand what you're saying, but I don't understand why."

He covered her tiny hand with his strong one. "I know. She asked that we keep everything she's doing a secret. A lot of it is a secret from me, and even your grandpa, your *jido*. She knows the three of us love her and she will tell us where she is when it's safe to do so. Until that happens we have no choice but to wait."

Hannah nodded in a solemn way and finally returned to her cookie.

7

R ebecca couldn't tear herself away from the crime scene neighborhood and continued to search for the Hawley children another two hours. Despite Sutter's warning, she went into several abandoned homes and buildings, constantly cautious about what might be in them. It bothered her that she hadn't run into any SVU inspectors as she searched.

Finally, she headed back to homicide.

To her surprise, Sutter wasn't at his desk. She tried calling, but his phone went straight to messaging. The department's administrative assistant, Elizabeth Havlin, said she saw him earlier that afternoon, but then he went out and hadn't returned.

Rebecca sat down to search what little street camera footage she had secured. Few security cameras had been set up in the area, and most of those were either broken or stolen.

She scrolled through the film, but Sutter's absence gnawed at her. After all, the man had been trying to track down a murderer. What if his investigation had turned up something, and he decided to pursue it on his own? If so, anything might have happened to him.

After a couple of hours of being unable to reach him by phone, she called Lt. Eastwood who had already left the office.

To her amazement, Eastwood told her Sutter needed to go home early that afternoon, but that he was fine.

Home? She couldn't understand why Bill Sutter would "need" to go home at a time like this. He was divorced, had no kids, lived in a small apartment, and his only pet was a goldfish. Why hadn't he told her what he was doing? And why didn't he answer her calls? It made no sense.

Richie strolled into Homicide after hours. As he expected, Rebecca was in the office alone. She looked up from her computer at the sound of his footsteps, and he loved the smile that lit her face at seeing him.

He couldn't stop himself from giving her a quick kiss, even though she hated displays of affection at work. But since no one else was around …

And she didn't seem to mind.

"I thought you'd be here," he said. He knew Rebecca and her partner were the on-call homicide team that week. It meant her time wasn't her own, and she was at the mercy of whatever cases dropped onto her lap. But it also meant she could be in danger. Perpetrators of homicides rarely went quietly when confronted. That meant Richie was on edge until he learned she was safely at home. "Have you had dinner yet?"

"I grabbed a sandwich a little while ago," she said, then drew in her breath. "Sutter and I have a new case, an ugly one."

"Oh?"

"A man was shot to death inside his home, and now his two kids are missing. They're only six and eight." He could see the worry on her face as she spoke of the children.

"Do you think the killer took them?" he asked.

"That's what worries us. I'm trying to find out all I can about the mother. She and the deceased recently separated. Sometimes when marriages go bad and there are kids, all kinds of terrible things can happen..."

He knew that, and didn't want to think about it. Didn't want *her* to think about it. "Why are you here alone?" he asked, changing the subject. "Where's Sutter?"

"He had to go home for some reason. Eastwood said I shouldn't worry about him."

Richie shook his head, then frowned. "And Eastwood's not worried because you do enough work for the both of you." He didn't care for her boss or her partner, but she wouldn't listen to criticism of them—at least not most of the time. "So, can I get you anything? Coffee? A candy bar?"

"No. I'm fine. I need to check a few databases, and I'm hoping to get some reports from forensics soon."

"Okay. I get the message. I'll get out of your hair." He was tempted to add that if she was willing to move in with him, they'd see each other later. But he didn't. One thing he'd learned about Rebecca, you couldn't pressure her into doing anything. She had a stubborn streak worse than his own.

She took his hand and drew him closer. "I liked that you stopped by. Thank you."

"That's because I love being with you—even when you give me the bum's rush."

"I didn't—"

"It's okay. Find those kids." He gave her a goodbye kiss, and heaved a sorrowful sigh as he left the bureau alone.

Sometimes, dating a homicide inspector sucked big time.

As he got into his Porsche, he remembered a call he'd gotten the day before from a potential client. He'd tried to blow the guy off, but he was insistent. Richie promised to call back and set up a meeting. That evening was as good as any.

He arranged a meeting with William Roland Allen at a neutral site—LaRocca's Corner, one of his favorite old-time San Francisco bars. There, whatever was said, whoever was met, should remain a secret. As Old Man LaRocca used to put it, "As we say in Sicilian, 'I don't know nothing about that too much.'"

And if you tried to tell what you'd learned there, it was said that the ghost of LaRocca would haunt you. Nobody wanted that.

Richie sat at a back booth, a draft pilsner in front of him, when an older fellow with elaborately styled snowy white hair entered the bar. He wore a dapper double-breasted pin-striped navy blue suit, white shirt and purple tie, and was thin to the point of boniness. He huddled near the door and looked completely baffled.

A cocktail waitress took pity on him. They spoke quietly, and then she pointed out the booth where Richie waited.

Richie stood as the fellow approached. "Mr. Allen?"

Allen looked around as if to make sure no one was listening, then quietly said, "Yes."

Richie held out his hand. "Richie Amalfi. Have a seat." He gestured toward one side of the booth and took his place opposite. "What will you have?" he asked as the waitress waited.

"I'll have a, um, cosmopolitan."

The waitress gave Richie a slight smile. He shrugged. This was more of a beer and a straight shot kind of place, not one that poured cranberry-based cocktails.

"So, Mr. Allen, what can I do for you?" Richie asked when they were alone.

Allen looked all but theatrical as he gripped the edge of the table. "I don't normally have this kind of problem, you see," Allen began then, as if realizing how he must appear, he folded his hands on the tabletop. "Please call me William."

William, not Bill, not Will, and definitely not Willie. Okay.

He cleared his throat and continued. "I'm an antiques dealer. Or, I was. I guess my difficulty began when I found a rare weathervane at a garage sale and purchased it for a song."

Richie stopped him. "A weathervane? You mean those things on barns?"

"And other structures, yes. Someone must have brought it to California years ago from a family farm back East because it isn't the sort of thing found or valued in San Francisco. It's late nineteenth century—a horse and rider in gilded copper, about thirty-three inches long."

Wake me when you're through. Richie was beginning to question his sanity at meeting this fellow before checking out what he was about.

"I thought it could be valuable," Allen continued, "so I had it appraised. It was valued, fifteen years ago, at thirty-thousand dollars."

That caught Richie's attention big time. "For a weathervane?"

"I'm afraid so." Allen ran a finger along his collar. "Over time, I grew fond of the piece. Extremely fond. So much so that when a customer wanted to buy it, I couldn't part with it. I kept putting him off while I had a copy made. I'm afraid I knew this customer too well. He'd put the piece in his den and show it off to people who couldn't tell a Ming vase from a Spode teapot."

"And now, the client has discovered he has a copy?"

Allen sucked in his cheeks. "Yes. That's part of it."

Richie waited for further explanation.

"After selling the copy, I waited to be caught, guilt-laden, for months. Nothing happened. Then, I did the same thing with another piece, and another. And I kept the originals for my own collection."

Richie picked up his beer. "How long have you been doing this?"

"Twelve years."

"*Twelve...*" Richie put the beer down again. "What's the name of your business?"

"It no longer exists. The antique business isn't quite what it used to be, and most so-called antique stores are nothing more than glorified indoor rummage sales."

Richie had to agree with that, but then he never was one for going to antique stores. If he wanted to see old furniture—which he didn't—all he had to do was to visit his mother who still had furniture and ceramic pieces once owned by her parents and grandparents. Many of the items had been made in Italy and shipped to this country by relatives long ago.

"So, what do you want from me?" Richie asked.

"Recently, antique prices jumped sky-high. I sold the original weathervane for fifty thousand dollars. That particular buyer was quite careful. I couldn't slip a fake past him. He also"—Allen's lips tightened—"liked publicity and let people know about his weathervane purchase. My earlier customer learned about it and realized he had a fake. He told a friend of his, another long-time customer, and now the two of them are threatening to create a fuss. I don't want a fuss. I'll gladly pay them back what they paid for the pieces."

"Did you offer that?"

"They won't take it."

"What do they want?"

"My head."

"And you've sold both your originals?" Richie asked.

"As I said, the price of antiques has jumped recently ..."

Richie leaned back against the booth seat and studied Allen a moment. Something about the guy and his story bothered him. But maybe it was just because the antique world was so different from Richie's. He could appreciate things, old and new, that were beautiful and valued for that beauty. But this guy and his story seemed as fake as a three-dollar bill.

"Have you offered to pay your customers what the pieces are worth now?"

"Well, no," Allen all but stuttered. "I had expenses. Lots of expenses. And I—"

"Would being paid current value satisfy them?" Richie demanded.

Allen seemed to ponder this a long while. "Possibly, but I'm not sure."

"That's could be a place to start," Richie suggested.

"But it's a lot of money!" Allen sounded almost angry.

"And if word got out to other customers that they'd been scammed, how much would you have to pay them? And would it keep you out of prison?"

Allen shut his eyes. "I understand all that," he admitted. "It's why I'm here."

Richie's eyes narrowed as he looked at the fellow. Sometimes, many times, he wondered why he bothered to help men like this. He took out his small leather-bound notepad and wrote down a ridiculously high number. To tell the truth, he saw it as a way to get "Willie" out of his life.

He handed the slip of paper to Allen. "My fee. If I'm not able to come to a satisfactory conclusion—namely, one that keeps you out of jail—I'll return all of it except five grand to cover time and expenses."

Allen gasped. "But this ... this is highway robbery!"

"No." Richie's voice was calm. "What you did was highway robbery. I'm just trying to keep the damage to a minimum. And, of course, I get paid first."

Allen stiffened, looking beyond indignant. But then, his face tight, he nodded. "I'll get you the money."

8

R ebecca was back at her desk the next morning before eight o'clock. As usual, she was the first detective to arrive at the bureau. The night before she had worked until two in the morning looking for information about Daryl Hawley as well as checking with the Special Victims Unit on the status of the search for Hawley's children.

She liked to stop at Peet's on her way to work for a cup of coffee and warm almond croissant. She bit into the croissant and sipped some coffee as she switched on her computer.

"Good morning."

She nearly choked on the coffee at the sound of Lieutenant Eastwood's voice. It took a moment before she could mumble a return greeting. Eastwood was never in the office that early. She couldn't help but gawk as he strode through the main bureau to his oversized private office.

Eastwood, age 49, was trim and fit, and spent several hours at the gym during the workweek. He dressed in expensive, conservative suits, and ninety-nine dollar cuts for his silvery hair weren't unheard of.

Rebecca wondered what was up. Not only did Eastwood

rarely arrive before nine, he never greeted the staff with more than a quick nod, if that.

Strange, she thought, and then turned to more important things, such as a wake-up call to SVU Inspector Cheryl Wong, who was heading up the search for Molly and Porter Hawley. Wong planned to visit the children's school that morning to see if she could learn anything more there, or if anyone had been hanging around them at school or as they played. Plus, they would check out any babysitters Tracy Hawley had hired.

As Rebecca hung up the phone, she saw the administrative assistant, Elizabeth Havlin, escorting a tall, handsome stranger to Eastwood's office. Elizabeth could scarcely take her gaze from the man and once walked into a chair that had been left too far out from a desk.

As Rebecca watched them, she understood Elizabeth's fascination. The fellow looked like he was in his early thirties, tall, 195 pounds or so, and appeared buff even in a charcoal suit and blue tie. From the neck up, he wasn't bad either, with gray eyes, light brown hair, and a well-chiseled face. She kept watching as the newcomer entered Eastwood's office.

Elizabeth quietly shut the door, then faced Rebecca and fluttered her hands in front of her face as if hot and bothered.

Rebecca waved her over. "Who is he?" she asked.

Elizabeth took a quick breath. "All I know is his name, Jared Woolridge. He asked for Eastwood and had a bunch of papers from Human Resources in his hand."

"Human resources?" Rebecca asked. Just then, two other homicide inspectors, Paavo Smith and Toshiro Yoshiwara, arrived, and Elizabeth returned to her office.

Paavo and Yosh had been working a complicated murder case for the past week. They were both grim-faced as the case seemed to have taken an ugly turn, and after a brief conversation with Rebecca about their case and her latest investigation, they left the office to conduct more interviews. Inspectors Luis Calderon and Bo Benson were off that day having worked the weekend shift and, as usual, Bill Sutter was late.

Rebecca told herself not to let Sutter irritate her. He was perpetually late. Still, she thought this case would have brought him to work on time. He had acted as if the missing kids bothered him as much as they did her. But she guessed not. She was ready to give up waiting for him and go back out in the field when her desk phone buzzed.

"The boss wants to see you," Elizabeth said breathlessly.

"In his office? Now?" Rebecca asked. She hadn't seen the stranger leave.

"That's right."

Curiouser and curiouser. Rebecca stood, smoothed her ivory turtleneck sweater, and made sure she had no croissant crumbs on her navy blue slacks.

Eastwood's office had become a running joke to the homicide inspectors. It once fit the position of the man occupying it, but when Eastwood realized he might have a chance of moving higher in the department, possibly to the position of chief of police, he seemed to think his office should reflect such aspirations. One day, his metal desk was out and a custom-built one of redwood burl put in its place. Such a desk needed a soft leather chair behind it. And visitors, particularly important visitors, shouldn't sit on hard chairs while Eastwood luxuriated, so his guest chairs became soft, matching armchairs. Plantation shutters hid the ugly view of the freeway overpass, and the staff was taking bets if he'd be able to persuade the building manager to put in hardwood floors.

"Come in," Eastwood called in response to her knock. As she entered, the lieutenant and the stranger stood. The old-world manners took her aback. Usually Eastwood scarcely acknowledged her when she entered his office and never rose.

"Rebecca," Eastwood said, "I'd like you to meet Homicide Inspector Jared Woolridge. Jared, this is Inspector Mayfield, one of the best on the squad, and she *had been* our newest detective."

Had been? That was unnerving. Puzzled, Rebecca looked from one man to the other.

Woolridge stood four or more inches over her five-foot-ten inch height. His brown eyes studied her as he held out his hand. "Hello."

"Inspector," she said, shaking his hand.

Woolridge stood before one guest chair and Eastwood gestured for Rebecca to take the other.

Eastwood faced her. "I'm sure you're wondering what this is all about. You can join me in congratulating Inspector Woolridge on his new assignment. He's here on detail from the Legal Division. Although nothing is finalized, there's a good possibility he'll be taking Bill Sutter's place."

Rebecca was beyond stunned. Her mind raced with the implications behind Eastwood's words. "I don't understand. Is Bill all right?"

Eastwood's gaze jumped to Woolridge a moment before answering. "He seems to have decided that the retirement he's been forever talking about needs to happen now."

"But that makes no sense—"

Eastwood raised his chin. "Maybe it's this case you've got. Missing kids. Probably dead. Who knows? He may have decided he can't handle it any longer."

She hated his flippant "probably dead" comment. She could feel her tension building as she tried to make sense of Bill's actions. "But Bill–"

"He asked to take a trial retirement to see how it feels." Eastwood had become the voice of reason. His words were firm, making clear that to ask any more questions would be a waste of time. "I'm sure once Bill tries retirement he'll love it."

"I suppose," she murmured. "I must admit I'm in shock."

"I'm sure you are," Eastwood said. "It came as a surprise to me, too, but this is as good a time as any for him to leave. He'll be available on call if we're desperate"—he smirked as if that would never be the case—"but he won't be around to talk to the press or anything like that."

Rebecca didn't like hearing that. Sutter loved to talk to the press and since she hated it, he always handled the PR side of their partnership. As she studied Eastwood, the more convinced she became that something was amiss. "I see," she said.

"No need to look so worried, Rebecca." Eastwood tried to laugh off the awkward silence. "I know you'll miss Bill. We all will. But, trust me, this change will be for the best. Now, why don't you take Jared out and introduce him to the others, find him a desk and all, and get to know him."

He waggled his fingers toward the door and waited for them to take the hint and leave.

"I'm so sorry, Inspector Woolridge," Rebecca said when they were alone in Homicide's now empty main room. "I'm afraid that wasn't much of a welcome. The sudden retirement of my partner shocked me."

"So I noticed," Woolridge said dryly.

"And you're coming to us from Legal? Isn't that part of Internal Affairs?"

Woolridge's mouth wrinkled. "I was afraid people might think that. We're both directly part of the police commissioner's staff, but that's it. The Legal division does mostly court liaison work, although we assist in defending the department. Or, I should say, that's what *they* do. Anyway, since I'm not a lawyer, promotional opportunities were limited over there. And besides, I wanted to get back to real police work."

"Can't say I blame you for that. And this position would be a lateral for you?"

"It would."

She nodded. People couldn't complain about that—not "officially" at any rate. Still, something felt off. It was no way to select a homicide inspector. The position was one of the highest ranking in prestige, if nothing else, in the SFPD's Investigations Division. She knew many career investigators in other departments who were waiting to pounce on an opening in Homicide.

She walked toward her desk. Woolridge followed, his gaze curious. "It seems everyone is out at the moment," she said.

"I imagine they're out investigating." Woolridge smiled at her.

"I'm sure they are." She looked around the room for a place to put the man.

He rubbed his palms together energetically. "To be honest, I can't wait to get started."

She knew she couldn't seat him at Sutter's desk. What if Sutter came into the bureau one day and found a new inspector sitting there? She had to admit that even though Sutter often drove her crazy, he was once a superb detective, and even now, he showed flashes of true ability. Also, he was a good man, even if he had a tendency to whine and do all he could to avoid handling anything difficult or dicey.

With Woolridge, rubbing his hands and looking ready to pounce on any and everything heading his way, she suspected her biggest problem might be reining him in. She couldn't help thinking if Hollywood ever showed up wanting someone to play the role of a homicide cop on a made-for-TV crime series, he would be perfect, right out of central casting. She wondered if that was what bothered her about him. He was young, enthusiastic, energetic, and handsome—which made him about as different from Bill Sutter as one could get.

"There's an empty desk," she said, heading toward a corner.

"It's not in a good location." She eyed the room. "Let's pull it out from the wall and make it a little more centered. I suspect Eastwood has given no thought to making you comfortable. He was probably too stunned at getting an immediate replacement for a retiring inspector."

"Believe me," Woolridge said as they pushed the desk, "I'm as surprised as anyone. I didn't even know there was an opening in this department. My boss knew I wanted to move to investigations and when he heard there might be an opening, he asked if I'd be interested. I didn't have to think about my answer which was, 'Absolutely!'"

"You were lucky," she said as she tried to think of which supplies and everything else Woolridge would need.

"You've got that right. He called back last night and told me to report this morning. I guess my detail will let us see if we're a good fit."

"The hours here are crazy. You didn't need to check with family?" she asked.

"Nope. No wife, no kids, and my folks live up around Shasta. I'm here on my own."

"I see." She couldn't help but think of how fast everything had come together. "You got a call yesterday, you said. What time was that?"

His brows crossed. "Why?"

"No reason."

"Around four."

"Incredible," she murmured. She didn't want to say anything to Woolridge, but that was only a few hours after Bill Sutter left her to return to Homicide to investigate Daryl Hawley. She just didn't get it.

He put his hands on his hips. "I see you're bothered. But look, this is just a temporary assignment. Your old partner might decide he hates being retired and comes back. I understood that was a possibility when I accepted the detail. But I want you to know I'll do everything I can to prove to everyone I'm able to do this job, and to be one of the best homicide inspectors this city has ever known."

Her eyebrows rose at his vehemence. She wasn't sure how to react and found herself making an awkward shrug as she murmured, "Fine."

He added, "I hope we can work well together, Inspector Mayfield."

Maybe she was being unfair taking her irritation at Sutter and the callous words of Eastwood out on this man. "Call me Rebecca," she said and then strode to the supply cabinet and pulled out notepads, pens and pencils for him. As always, he followed.

"And please call me Jared," he added as he held out his hands to take the supplies she gathered.

She eyed him, then gave a small smile. "Okay, Jared. We'll need to talk to Elizabeth about getting you a cell phone and computer."

She was sliding a desk chair into place for Woolridge when Lt. Eastwood approached.

"Looks like you two are getting along and making progress," he said.

"Yes, we are," Rebecca said. No thanks to you, she wanted to add. "But now that Jared has a desk, we've got to get working the Hawley case. I came up with a few things last night I want to check on."

Eastwood nodded. "Excellent. Well, have fun, you two."

Fun? Rebecca cringed. What a jerk.

9

V ito Grazioso was up early that morning and drove to the mayor's home, parking a half-block away. Along with most of the city's wealthiest politicians, Mayor Cornelius Warren lived in a beautiful early twentieth century mansion in the Presidio Heights area.

To surveil in that location, Vito used his wife's compact Mazda, figuring the car would be a lot less noticeable than his big GMC truck, and passersby would think it belonged to some member of a help staff.

Vito's wife didn't mind him using it. With five kids, she pretty much always drove their minivan.

Mayor Cornelius Warren had a reputation for not being an early riser, so Vito felt fairly certain the mayor was still home. Using a camera with a powerful telephoto lens, he could photograph anyone who came or went, and later determine who the person was.

At eight-thirty, a man—butler or security guard Vito guessed —opened the front door, picked up the morning *Chronicle* from the door stoop, and then went back inside. After that, absolutely nothing happened until ten when a black Mercedes sedan pulled up to the garage. Mayor Warren walked out of the house and hurried to the car. Vito marveled at the man's appearance. Vito wasn't one for watching local news on TV, or national for that matter. He had enough to worry about with five kids and Richie, and he wasn't sure which caused him the most trouble. Still, he remembered what Cornelius Warren used to look like. The guy had gone from being short, pudgy, and balding to having lost at least fifty pounds and was now wearing an expensive toupee. Obviously, he was planning to run for higher office.

Vito followed the mayor's vehicle to the VIP garage under City Hall. To enter, Vito pulled out his City Hall parking pass, one of many specialty passes he'd accumulated to do his job. He parked several stalls away from the mayor.

An hour and a half went by before the mayor got into his car again and Vito followed him across the city to the Olympic Club. Another of Vito's many passes let him into the parking lot, despite the way the parking attendant sneered at his Mazda.

To Vito, it seemed the mayor was going to play a little golf, and probably afterward visit the Nineteenth Hole or whatever they called the bar in a posh setting like this one.

Vito returned to his car, to the thermos of coffee and the packed lunch his wife had made for him. She understood the rigors of surveillance.

As the mayor's foursome headed out to the links, Vito phoned Shay.

"Am I wasting my time here?" Vito asked, his voice morose.

"You know the drill. Establish the routine, and then you'll know when the mark has deviated from it," Shay said.

"Sleep, eat with donors, play with donors, drink with donors, then go back home to sleep again. I think that's what I'm going to find."

"It's only day one," Shay said, but Vito could hear the skepticism in his voice.

"I take it you're not having any better luck," Vito said.

"I just started going through Hiz Honor's finances. Lots of hanky-panky with political donations, but I'd be more shocked if I didn't see any. But it's early yet."

"What's Richie up to?"

"All I've heard is he's trying to take his mind off all this by working with some loser who scammed people with fake antiques. After just one meeting, the guy is already driving him crazy."

"You got a name?"

"Richie won't give it. Said he's not important—protecting Rebecca is. He doesn't want us involved. I suspect antique dealers aren't particularly dangerous people."

Vito smirked. "I hope not. But the way the world is going, who knows anymore.

Rebecca and Jared arrived at the Hawley house in separate cars, just as she and Sutter would have done. She wanted Jared to see the crime scene, and she also wanted to look around the house, particularly at Daryl Hawley's papers and such without the distraction of crime scene technicians and the medical examiner's team.

Crime scene tape cordoned off the house, with signs warning people to keep out. Rebecca had a key and unlocked the door. The inside looked very much the way it had when she left the day before with fingerprint dusting powder on doorjambs, window sills, and elsewhere. She and Jared slowly passed through the living room, again looking for anything that could give them a lead, and entered the kitchen. There, she pointed out where Daryl Hawley's body had lain, giving him a condensed version of all she knew so far.

"I'm going to check out the bedrooms," Jared said, pulling a pair of disposable gloves from his pocket, leaving Rebecca alone beside the dried blood left behind when Hawley's body was taken away.

Something about the house felt off. And it wasn't because a man had died there. Rebecca felt as if someone was watching her, as if someone other than Jared was near. Her hand went to her gun, holstered against the back of her waist, under her jacket. She didn't pull it out. Not yet.

She moved toward the small porch just past the kitchen. The door to the backyard had glass in the upper half. She peered through it guardedly. The large yard was unkempt with weeds, high, overgrown bushes, and enclosed by a rickety wood fence. She thought she saw some kind of movement through the bushes and drew her gun as she opened the back door. All seemed quiet.

She cautiously stepped through the door, but as she did a shot rang out. She dived back into the house for cover. A man, lithe, wearing a dark hoodie and blue jeans, hurled himself over the back fence and dropped out of sight.

She ran to the fence and boosted herself up so she could see over it. "Stop!" she yelled, seeing the shooter as he rounded the house just behind Hawley's. "Police! Stop or I'll shoot!"

He had already disappeared, but she didn't let that stop her. She was about to raise herself up and over the fence, when she heard another gunshot, this one from her right. There was another house there, another yard.

She dropped back down, crouching low, her heart pounding from fear and adrenaline.

Staying down, she ran behind a bush, then half-scurried, half-crawled in the direction the second shot had come from, stopping only when she reached cover behind the side fence.

"Rebecca!" Jared stood in the back doorway, his gun drawn. "Are you all right?"

"Get down! Active shooter. Two of them."

"Two?" He bent low and ran toward her. No gunfire sounded. "Are you sure?"

"I'm sure! The second shot came from the other side of this fence. Whoever shot at me is probably gone now, but let's see what we can find."

They ran from Hawley's house to the house next door. The front and back yards were empty, with no sign of anyone having been in the yard. The house, which Rebecca knew was vacant, remained locked, the windows closed. There wasn't a soul around.

Rebecca stood, hands on hips, furious she had lost the shooters.

"I don't understand this," Jared said. "Why would a second person be shooting at you from the house next door? Maybe you heard wrong—a bullet ricocheted, and you thought the shot came from your right side when it didn't."

"I know what I saw and heard. The guy I was chasing went over the back fence to the next yard. He had just disappeared behind the house when someone fired at me from my right side. There was no way the first shooter could have done that. There wasn't enough time."

"I'm going to call Eastwood," Jared said, "tell him about the shootings, and get some crime scene techs out here to find the bullets."

"Eastwood can wait," Rebecca said, making sure he knew she was the lead on this investigation. "I didn't fire my weapon, neither did you, so there's no need for an immediate report. Let's look around first, see what, if anything, we can find before getting the techs here."

"You always play fast and loose?" Jared asked.

"Only when I need to."

Something was definitely wrong with this shooting, but she didn't feel the need to voice that feeling to Jared. She also didn't voice her other lingering thought. Had she become a target?

~

Richie was home, pacing. He hadn't heard anything so far that day from Rebecca, Shay or Vito, and the silence bothered him. He wanted to talk more to Rebecca about his worries concerning her job, the people at City Hall, and the danger she was in. He couldn't help but think—yet again—if they'd been living together, he could have done it. But they weren't … and he really needed to stop thinking about it! Besides, she was busy with her latest case, so talking to her about his anxiety would have to wait. *Damn!*

Still, he could feel in his bones that something was very wrong. He couldn't pinpoint it; all he knew was it was making him increasingly nervous.

He'd tried to distract himself from worrying about Rebecca by doing an internet search for William Roland Allen. He found nothing that fit the age or occupation of the man he'd met.

Even on private eye networks he belonged to—those sites where personal information could be gotten for a price—nothing matched.

Richie had gotten a bad feeling while talking to Allen. Now, that feeling multiplied.

He'd given Willie forty-eight hours to get the money together. Willie was supposed to call with the location to meet. There, Richie would get his payment, plus the names of the two men trying to, essentially, blackmail Willie. Once he had those names, he'd get to work.

The whole business of thieves vs. thieves was par for the course. What wasn't common, however, was not being able to trace his client.

Giving up, however, wasn't an option. He never gave up. On anything.

10

The house next to Daryl Hawley's was empty, and from what Rebecca and Jared saw, it had been empty for a year or more. The only thing alive in it were rats. If the second shooter had been hiding inside, he'd left no trace behind.

She knew Jared was anxious to call in the shooting and to get a CSI team out to comb both yards for bullet casings and bullets, but Rebecca needed to handle this her own way.

The instant they were back in the Hawley home, Rebecca walked straight to the kitchen and to the door where she'd been standing when the first bullet had been fired at her. It didn't take much looking. The bullet was lodged in the door frame, just inches away from where she'd been standing. Seeing how close it had been to her head was unnerving.

After Jared took photos with his cell phone, she took out a pocket knife and dug out the wood where the bullet had lodged, to keep from messing up any markings on the slug, and placed it in an evidence bag. She couldn't help but wonder if it was from the same gun that killed Daryl Hawley.

And if so, why had the shooter returned to the scene of the

crime? Was it to find something there that he needed or had left behind?

And who was the second shooter? Was he there to keep watch? To warn the 'inside man' that someone was approaching?

Those thoughts made her wonder, yet again, if she was the target. And if so, why?

She pushed that to the back of her mind, and got back to the Hawley investigation.

Confirming what the crime scene investigators had determined yesterday, she and Jared found nothing in the Hawley house that seemed suspicious. No drugs. No guns. A six-pack of beer in the fridge. Nothing stronger. It was time to move on.

She and Jared next went to Daryl Hawley's place of employment, RX Wholesale, a medical supply center that stocked surgical supplies, equipment, vaccines, and pharmaceuticals for delivery to healthcare practitioners and doctors. The warehouse was located in the southeastern most part of the city near the Bayshore freeway, a good spot to make pharmaceutical deliveries throughout the Bay Area.

Raymond McKennan confirmed that Hawley had worked there for five years. He was an okay worker, with little ambition and little drive. He seemed content to drive a truck and never asked about advancement. All that was fine with McKennan. He implied Hawley didn't have the brains to handle much more than he was doing.

"How did he get along with his co-workers and people on his route?"

"Everyone seemed to like him well enough, although he didn't have much to do with anybody. Oh..." McKennan blurted out the word, then seemed to think better of it, and shut his mouth.

"Oh?" Rebecca asked.

"It's probably nothing."

"You can tell me," she said.

"All I can say is the troubles with his wife changed Hawley. He was always quiet, but became even more of a loner and far less friendly and open than he once had been. Still, he's not a guy I'd ever imagine as a murder victim. I mean, why? There was nothing to the man. He was a good worker with a strong back. Some pieces of medical equipment we deliver are darn heavy. We were happy to have him."

What an epitaph, Rebecca thought. She asked about problems with alcohol or drugs.

"I guess he enjoyed a beer now and then. But it never interfered with his job."

With that, she asked McKennon for the names of any co-workers who were friends with Hawley. After getting two names, she thanked McKennon and left.

Rebecca sent Jared off to talk to the co-workers and anyone they could suggest who knew Hawley, while she drove to Tracy Hawley's apartment in the Sunset district. Tracy's sister opened the door. Tracy had been given some tranquilizers and was still sleeping. Between finding Daryl dead and her children missing, Tracy couldn't stop crying, and the doctor decided that was the only way to enable her to rest. They also hoped she would wake to good news.

So far, that wasn't the case.

"What's your name?" Rebecca asked the sister.

"Pam Reynolds."

"Do you live nearby?"

"In Modesto. Tracy called and told me what was going on. She wanted to make sure our parents didn't hear about it and want to come and stay with her. They live in Nebraska and wouldn't know how to handle any of this. We rarely see them anymore."

"Do you see Tracy often?"

"No. I have three kids and a job of my own. They keep me busy. My husband is watching them while I'm here."

"Did you know Tracy and Daryl were separated?"

"Sure. I'm surprised it didn't happen sooner. The guy's a loser. I mean, I guess I shouldn't speak ill of the dead, but he was. I don't know what Tracy saw in him. Although … she's older than Daryl. Thirty-five when they married—he was twenty-eight or so—and I think she felt it was him or no one. The best thing from that marriage is their kids. I can't believe they're missing!"

"We're doing our best," Rebecca said. "Did you ever hear anything that might indicate why someone would want Daryl dead? Anyone he or Tracy argued with? Any boyfriend of Tracy's, or even a jealous girlfriend of Daryl's?"

As she spoke, Pam shook her head and kept shaking it. "I've thought about it. But, honestly, I don't know why anyone would want to bother to kill him."

"Thanks," Rebecca said. *With friends like these…* She couldn't help but hope Daryl Hawley hadn't suspected the way most people seemed to regard him.

As Rebecca pulled into the drive-through line at McDonald's, she tried not to think about those two bullets that had been aimed straight at her. She had no one to talk to about it, not her old partner, and certainly not her new one. And she certainly didn't want to tell Richie who was already spending too much time worrying about her.

Still, she'd give anything to, right now, be sitting down with Richie at The Leaning Tower Taverna, sharing a bottle of wine, and forgetting that someone had tried to kill her.

But such thoughts had no place in her mind at the moment. Figuring out why Hawley had been killed, and by whom, was her top priority. Her only priority, in fact. Doing that, she hoped, would help to find his two children.

She picked up her order, and headed back to the Hall of Justice.

Once there, she turned over the bullet she'd retrieved to Ballistics and asked them to put a rush on comparing it to the one that killed Hawley. From there she went to Homicide and sat at her desk, munching on her now cold burger, and tried to track down any of Daryl Hawley's relatives.

There were none in the area. His parents were dead. She found a cousin in Las Vegas, but he could tell her nothing. Looking around Hawley's house, he didn't appear to have had any close family members.

She also checked with the computer techs to see if anything interesting turned up on Hawley's computer. It looked as if he used it for video games and ordering from Amazon.

As she searched through his files, she became aware of someone standing beside her.

She looked up. Lieutenant Eastwood.

"When were you going to tell me about it?" he asked, a deep frown marring his face.

She knew exactly what he was talking about. "I've written out a report. Nothing happened. Neither Jared or I fired our weapons. Someone was lurking in the Hawley yard. He shot at me. I went after the shooter, but someone else took another shot at me. I wasn't hit, but by the time Jared reached me and we began to search, we could find no trace of either person."

"What did the shooters look like?"

"The first wore a hoodie, jeans, and white running shoes. He had to be young and spry the way he went over the fence running away from me, but that's as much as I can say. I never saw the person who fired from the side. I did retrieve the first bullet.

Ballistics has it and they're checking the marking to see if it came from the same gun that—"

Her cell phone rang. She glanced at the number. "That's Ballistics now," she said.

"Take the call," he said.

She listened to the woman on the other end, an expert in the field. The bullet found in the doorframe did not match the one that killed Daryl Hawley.

Rebecca found herself gritting her teeth. The number of shooters and guns involved just grew. She relayed the news to her boss.

Eastwood's face grew impassive, but his words were instantaneous. "We'll send some crime scene techs out there to see if they can find the second bullet fired at you. I want to know more about it."

Finally, Rebecca thought, something they could agree on. She wanted to more as well.

A little before six that evening, Jared returned. He gave Rebecca the list of Hawley's friends that he'd tracked down. "None of them had anything to say," he told her. "Daryl was just a regular guy, kind of dull, he did nothing much but work. He was devoted to his kids. When his wife told him she was leaving him, he didn't even try to fight her. He said he was surprised a woman like her would put up with him as long as she had. He saw her as beautiful, intelligent, and with a good job. But his friends seemed to find her average looking, not especially bright, and bossy and mean to Daryl."

"Do they think she could be behind his murder?"

"No. They all said she wouldn't have given him that much time or attention."

A shudder went down Rebecca's back. All she could think of was what a miserable marriage it had to have been.

Around seven that evening, Rebecca turned to Jared. "I'm starving. I'm going to head home, feed my dog, and get a quick bite to eat. I'll be back in an hour, but you can call it quits for the day. You probably have a lot of things to take care of, changing jobs so quickly. If you need to go back to Legal for anything, feel free."

"I'm fine," he said. "I want to see this through and find those kids as much as you do. I think I'll stay and search a few of Hawley's friends in our databases. I came across some weird characters today."

"Okay. Be back soon." Rebecca felt odd leaving a partner who was still working. It had almost never happened with Sutter. She told herself to appreciate Jared, but the timing of his getting the detail to Homicide still bothered her.

Rebecca hurried to her apartment. She had no sooner stepped in the door and was greeting Spike, her little Chinese Crested Hairless mix dog, when she received a call from the object of many of her thoughts that day, Bill Sutter.

"Rebecca, I'm right outside your apartment. I need to talk to you."

"Bill, my God," she cried, shocked but glad to hear from him. "I'll open the door."

Her apartment was in a three-story tall building that had one apartment on the second floor and one on the third, and a garage on the ground floor. Rebecca's tiny apartment was a converted storeroom off the back of that garage. The good part was that it faced the backyard which Rebecca thought of as her own private patio. The bad part was that to get to it a person had to go through a dark breezeway that ran along the side of the garage and then across the backyard to her apartment door.

She dashed down the breezeway to the outer door that stood between it and the sidewalk.

A bedraggled-looking Bill Sutter waited there. In his late fifties, he was rather young to think about retirement, but he had put in more than enough years on the police force to qualify. His gray hair was clipped short, and the most remarkable thing about his long face were the multiple bags under his eyes.

She didn't know what to say to him. Congratulations came to mind, but he didn't look like he was at all happy. "I was going to phone you this evening," she said, realizing she should have found time to call earlier.

"It's okay," he muttered as he stepped past her. He'd been to her apartment many times over the years. Once inside, he bent over to greet Spike with a brisk head rubbing which the little dog enjoyed. Spike had always liked Bill.

Finally, he straightened and faced Rebecca. His eyes were troubled, his whole being seemed deflated, as if he were much smaller, almost cadaverous, than he had seemed the day before. One glance at his expression told her he was as unsure of what to say as she was.

She took the initiative. "What's going on, Bill?"

He took off his overcoat, laid it on the sofa, and then crossed the room to the small dinette and sat. "That's why I'm here."

"Would you like coffee or anything?" she asked. "A beer, maybe?"

"Beer sounds good." He waited a moment as she took two bottles from the fridge and opened them. Then, his voice gruff, he said, "I know I've talked forever about retiring, but I never thought I'd be pushed out."

That was the last thing she expected to hear. She handed him a beer and took a seat across from him at the table. "Impossible. You? What do you mean?"

He took a long swallow. "Yesterday, soon after I returned to Homicide, I got a call from the police commissioner's administrative aide. She said Barcelli wanted to see me." Sutter ran a hand over his rubbery face. She had never noticed how thin his hands were. "I thought it was for something good. A pat on the back, maybe even a commendation for all the years I've served. No such luck. Instead, he told me there's a problem with a case, one you and I worked on together."

Rebecca had heard nothing about such a problem. "Which case?"

"Sharon Lynch's murder."

Rebecca's breath caught. But soon her teeth clenched as details of all that took place washed over her.

"Why, in God's name, does the police commissioner care about that case now?" she asked hotly.

Sutter's jaw clenched a moment. "Virginia Kirk has decided to sue the city because it continues to allow two insensitive, prejudiced people to work for the police department. Namely, you and me."

Rebecca gasped. "You've got to be kidding."

One Saturday morning, two years earlier, Sharon Lynch, a social worker, had been found dead in her apartment from trauma to the head. Neighbors and co-workers all knew that she and her roommate, Virginia Kirk, didn't get along at all.

Kirk, an accounting clerk at City Hall, claimed she had left San Francisco on Friday evening to drive to Reno, Nevada, where she enjoyed seeing shows and gambling. She was there when, the next day, she received a call from the police telling her someone had murdered her roommate.

Kirk had told several co-workers that she was planning a trip to Reno that weekend. The odd thing, however, was that she had never before discussed such plans with them. To Rebecca, it all seemed premeditated—as if she were setting up an alibi.

Neighbors claimed to have heard arguing coming from her apartment and believed they had heard her voice. There was no evidence of a break-in, and the deceased, Sharon Lynch, had told her coworkers she would spend the evening at home making popcorn and watching movies. She had added that her ridiculous roommate would probably complain about her choice of movies, just as she complained about everything else. But Sharon would watch what she wanted, no matter what.

"The case was as clear as anything can be when there aren't eye-witnesses," Rebecca said. "The roommates hated each other, and Kirk killed her."

"She was guilty," Sutter said. "But we lost in court."

Rebecca frowned. "We did." Her gaze lifted to Sutter's with sympathy. "And because of that you were asked to leave your job?"

"Not exactly. Commissioner Barcelli said if I took my retirement, Kirk's lawyers would drop the charges against me and I could slip away. No one is interested in going after my pension. It was my choice, but if I were to remain on duty, they would go after me for damages. And since I've been thinking about retiring …"

This bothered her—especially as she thought about Jared being assigned to Sutter's position within minutes, it seemed, of this conversation with the commissioner. She debated telling Sutter about her conversation with Jared, but she wasn't sure how he would handle it. She decided to wait and give Sutter a chance to get over the emotional toll this was taking on him. She switched gears. "How can it be that no one has said a word about Virginia Kirk's lawsuit?"

"I've been wondering the same thing." Sutter looked even more hangdog than ever. "It's obvious they offered me a way out because they want you to be the fall guy, or worse. Be warned, if the city shifts the blame onto you, they'll let you go and you'll have to fight the charges on your own."

His words stunned her. "There's no way I can afford an attorney good enough to defend against all that."

"Tell me about it. Why do you think I retired? And fast. I was out before I could even give the news people the scoop on the missing kids and their photos. Goddamn lawyers."

The thought of such a lawsuit made her entire body feel cold and shaky. Anger also stirred at the loss of time in getting word out about the missing kids.

Just then, she heard a knock on her door.

Only three people could get past the outer door that led to the breezeway—her upstairs neighbors, Kiki and Bradley, or the man she'd given a key to, Richie Amalfi.

She opened the door. Relief filled her. She threw her arms around a stunned Richie, gave him a quick kiss, and held him tight. "Thank God you're here!"

11

Hours passed with Porter and Molly alone in the dark. Porter wanted to walk around, even though there wasn't a glint of light in the room, but Molly was too scared.

He'd take a few steps at a time, then they'd talk, afraid of losing each other in the nothingness.

Porter froze at the sound of a key in the door. Then it opened and light entered the basement. Porter rubbed his eyes, the sudden light nearly blinding him.

"Don't move. Don't try to come up the stairs… or else," the man standing in the doorway said, his words little more than a whisper, but they echoed around the room. Molly huddled in the center of the room, crying. Porter shivered where he stood—close to the dolls, and looking at them now, he shivered even more.

They looked like real children, not dolls, sitting at two sets of tables and chairs, all small, like he had used in kindergarten class.

The man had told him and Molly not to move, so he didn't. He could tell the man was putting food at the top of the stairs again. He thought about rushing up the stairs and tackling him, but he knew that was crazy. He was too little and the man was so big.

He eased further from the man, but that brought him closer to the dolls.

There were four of them. They looked alive, but they couldn't be.

All had short black hair, and faces with red streaks that ran from their eyes down their cheeks. They looked like tears. Or blood.

He didn't like the dolls. Not at all. But he was glad they were dolls and not real children. Because if they were kids, staying that still and quiet meant they were dead.

With that thought, he couldn't stand being close to them another minute.

Ignoring the man's words to stay still, he rushed over to Molly and held her close, for her comfort and his own.

The man spoke again. "I'm leaving now. I've left you food. And you, boy, I saw you looking at my dolls. Don't do it. And if you want to live, don't touch them. Ever!"

He turned and walked out.

"Wait! Stop!" Porter and Molly screamed, and in the last of the outside light, they ran up the stairs after him. But he was gone. The door was shut. They tried to open it, but it was locked and the basement once again was blacker than night.

They sat at the top of the stairs, both crying, scared and hungry. They forced themselves to eat the food he'd left behind. After wiping away tears, and eating their fill, they carefully descended the stairs. Staying close to the walls, Porter led the way as they circled the basement. They found the panel with the buttons for the platform, but no matter how many times they pushed the buttons, the platform refused to move.

They continued on. Stacks of heavy boxes lined the walls along with an occasional coffin. Porter and Molly went around them, doing their best to stay near walls and hoping to find another door, maybe a window, or even an air vent big enough for them to crawl through. But they had no such luck.

Before long they reached an area where they felt cloth, and then the fake hair, plastic arms and hands and faces of the dolls. Porter thought about how odd it was that they were dolls that looked like school-aged little girls. They weren't the adult-looking Barbies that Molly liked to play with, or even baby dolls like she played with when she was younger. Porter wondered why the man had so many dolls, and why they all looked so strange.

He didn't like thinking about it, and something made him grip Molly's hand even tighter.

As they continued along the walls, Porter reached what felt like a switch. He flicked it up, and the lights came on. He almost wished they hadn't.

12

As Richie walked into Rebecca's apartment, his astonished gaze jumped from her to Bill Sutter. The tension in the room was so heavy he could all but taste it. "What's going on?"

"I was just leaving. Rebecca will tell you all about it." Sutter gave her a hug as he said goodbye.

Richie was now even more shocked. Rebecca and Sutter didn't have a hugging-type relationship. Most days she seemed ready to shoot the guy. He studied Rebecca as she saw Sutter to the door. She looked frazzled and tired. Even her large blue eyes, usually lively and sparkling, had lost their sheen. He expected tired—he knew she always put in long hours at the start of any homicide investigation since the first three days were often the most productive for finding the perpetrator. After that, murders became increasingly difficult to solve.

But the frazzled look worried him. Something was bothering her deeply, and apparently, Bill Sutter as well.

He stepped close to her, searching her face. "What's wrong?"

She faced him, then ran a hand against her hair, smoothing it and tucking blond flyaway strands behind her ears. She took a deep breath. "Something strange is going on at work."

He took her hand and drew her close. "Your case? Did you learn something about the missing kids?" His voice was soft, gentle.

"No. Nothing new with the case, or with the kids." She seemed lost in thought.

"Something about Sutter?" he asked, thinking about their strange parting.

She nodded, then headed to the kitchen. "Let me make myself a sandwich to take back to work as I tell you about it." She pulled some sliced ham, cheese, and mayonnaise from the refrigerator. "I was about to make one when Sutter showed up."

"Why did he come here?" Richie helped her by taking two slices of rye bread from the loaf and putting them on a plate. "Won't you see him tonight?"

She stilled, then murmured, "He retired."

"No way." Richie put down the loaf of bread and stared at her. "Sutter's the type who loves to talk about retiring some day, but would never actually do it. He's not sick or anything, is he? Come to think of it, he looked a little pale."

"No. It's nothing physical." She began to make the sandwich.

His head cocked. "Oh?"

She put down the knife she was using to spread the mayonnaise. "He was pressured into leaving." He could hear emotion in her voice over the injustice done to her colleague.

She told him about the conversation Sutter had had with the police commissioner and his warning about the upcoming civil case against her.

"I vaguely remember that case," Richie said. "It happened before I knew you, but it sounded like Ginny Kirk was guilty, and then some proof came in that she wasn't."

"That was the story in the press," Rebecca said. "Our investigation pointed to Virginia Kirk losing patience with a horrible roommate that she couldn't get rid of. Based on tenant's rights in the city, one roommate can't insist the other roommate move if the other doesn't want to. Sharon Lynch, the victim, was chronically late paying her share of the rent and other bills, took Kirk's clothes without permission, and even spent time with the man Kirk had a crush on."

"A man?" Richie asked. "But I thought ..."

"Exactly. Simply because the case involved two single women, some activists decided that they were in 'a relationship' with each other and, because of that, they said the homophobic police were railroading Kirk, or 'poor Ginny' as they called her. God, how I'd love to forget all that ugliness!"

"As if anyone in this city would have cared what kind of relationship they had," Richie said.

"Still, just the allegations were enough to cause the district attorney to lower the charge from second-degree murder to 'involuntary manslaughter.'" Rebecca folded her arms as more details came rushing back at her. "No one wanted to pay any attention to the forensic evidence we found."

"What was that evidence?" Richie asked, realizing how little actual evidence he'd ever heard about the case.

"We believe the two women argued, the argument had gotten out of hand, and then Kirk grabbed a cast-iron skillet and slammed it against the side of Sharon's head. As Sharon went down, she hit her head against the edge of the granite countertop. With those one-two blows, she died quickly."

"Wait, it's coming back now," Richie said. "Wasn't Kirk proven to be out of town? Isn't that why she got off?"

"Actually, there was no evidence that Virginia Kirk arrived in Reno before midnight when she checked into a hotel, which easily gave her time to kill Sharon, clean up the kitchen, and then drive to Reno," Rebecca pointed out. "But the press pushed the theory that Sharon let a stranger into the apartment and that's who really killed her."

"And that wrecked your case?" Richie asked. "Press coverage?"

"Not exactly," Rebecca said. "It fell apart when a woman, a so-called concerned citizen, showed up with a photograph of Virginia Kirk sitting at a slot machine in Harrah's and the wrist-watch on the person next to her showed it was nine o'clock. But was it a.m.? Or p.m.? Maybe Greenwich Mean Time? No way to tell in a casino. This woman, allegedly a stranger with no connection to the case, swore she just happened to be there taking pictures on the night of the murder. Give me a break!"

"Most cameras have date and time stamps," Richie said.

"Not old ones," Rebecca said. "And that's what she was using. For all we knew, the photo could have been taken while 'poor Ginny' was out on bail."

"So she was found not guilty."

"Actually, the chicken-shit DA didn't want to chance taking the case to court. We had to release her."

Richie understood Rebecca's fury. "Justice wasn't served."

"Not at all," she said. "Sutter and I got pummeled from all sides. The press accused us of being biased against Kirk, and people on Sharon Lynch's side were yelling at us for letting her murderer go free. Fortunately, Sutter enjoyed dealing with the press, not so much with Lynch's relatives, but he handled it all well enough. The whole thing was a hot mess."

Richie shook his head. "A real triumph for sensational journalism and spines of mush politicians. And now, I guess it's not the first time a suspect has sued for wrongful arrest."

Rebecca turned back to finishing her sandwich and putting it into a zip-lock plastic bag. At the same time, he watched her emotions go from sorrow to anger. "I don't get it. Why isn't the brass fighting this suit? Sutter and I did nothing wrong! What's wrong with these people?"

"Let me see what I can find out," he offered.

She shook her head. "I doubt you—"

"Really?" He raised his eyebrows.

"I take that back," she said with a smile, and he was glad to see her smiling again. "Maybe you can learn something. Right now, I've got to go back to Homicide. They've given me a rookie partner, his first time working a homicide. I need to make sure he doesn't mess anything up."

"A new partner already?" He knew enough about bureaucracies to be sure of three things about them. They moved slower than molasses; their actions always had an ulterior motive; and he never, ever, wanted to work in one.

"Strange, isn't it?" she said.

He waited as she locked up the apartment and then they walked out to the street. When she reached her SUV, he placed his hand on her arm. "Be careful out there and don't let this potential lawsuit distract you from being vigilant. Suits are usually settled long before going to court."

Her blue eyes met his dark ones. "If I get sued and the department and the union both bail on me, I could end up in debt for the rest of my life."

"Look at the bright side," he said as he moved closer, a slight smile crinkling the outer corners of his eyes. "At least with me here, you won't be homeless."

For just a moment she paused in her rush to get back to work and looked up at him, really looked at this complex man who had opened his heart and now his home to her. She took in his dark eyes, firm lips, and the wavy black hair she loved to run her fingers through. No matter what happened, from the time they met, he was always there for her.

Thoughts of the bullet that came so close to her that morning swept over her, and the realization of how much she had to lose. She couldn't help but shudder and hoped he didn't notice. She didn't want to tell him about it. He already spent far too much time worrying about her, and this would only add to his fears about her job.

"Tomorrow night," she whispered as she wrapped her arms around him and gave him a quick but heartfelt kiss. "I'll do everything I can to spend time with you."

～

Richie hated leaving Rebecca, considering this new development in her life. He had to do something, and he already had an idea in mind.

With that thought, he drove to Big Caesar's, his North Beach nightclub. The club was still doing well and bringing in a healthy profit at the end of each month, much to his surprise. He had bought Big Caesar's almost as a lark, but people seemed to enjoy the posh setting and older dance music they played. Once he got into the whole "dance club" scene, he discovered that adding music and songs from the "neo-swing" bands like Big Bad Voodoo Daddy, the Brian Setzer Orchestra, and the Royal Crown Revue, made the club more popular than ever.

He parked in his reserved spot in the back alley and went inside. He stuck his head in the main ballroom to make sure everything was fine. It was. The latest band he'd hired was warming up to "Hey Pachuco!" He scarcely heard the horns or drumbeat in the music. He was too upset over all that was happening to Rebecca. And not happening between them because of it.

He went to the office and put in a conference call to Shay and Vito.

"A slight change in emphasis," Richie said. "I need you both to look into what's going on with a woman named Virginia Kirk. You might remember the Sharon Lynch murder case a couple of years back. Kirk was charged with the murder but then new evidence turned up and she was released. Rebecca was the arresting officer and now Kirk wants to sue her saying that the charges were false and the arrest a bad one."

"I remember the case," Shay said. "Rebecca shouldn't have to worry."

"Normally, no, but the police commissioner scared off her old partner. If he quietly takes his retirement like a good boy, the top brass will see he isn't brought into the case. That means if he does anything to help her, his pension will be on the line. And she knows it. This case could mean she'll lose her job, and going to court, even if she won, would cost a small fortune. As far as I'm concerned, if she were no longer a cop that'd be a good thing, but only if it's *her* choice. Right now, she loves what she does, and doesn't want to leave it."

"And she's a good cop," Vito said. "But I don't trust her current or prior bosses."

"I want to know who Virginia Kirk has been talking to lately," Richie continued. "Who's her attorney? Has she had any contacts with anyone inside the police department or City Hall this past month? Same for her attorney. This whole thing stinks."

13

T he next morning, Rebecca arrived at Homicide after only four hours of sleep. Finding Jared already at his desk surprised her. It didn't surprise her that ever-efficient Elizabeth sat with him helping him set up his computer.

"Good morning," Rebecca said. "I didn't expect you here so early."

"I wanted to get my computer running." He glanced from Rebecca to Elizabeth. "And I heard Liz is often the first one here in the morning. I knew I could count on her to help me."

He flashed Elizabeth a smile that nearly caused her to swoon on the spot. She might be some fifteen years his senior, but she wasn't immune to his looks.

And Rebecca had never heard anyone call her Liz before.

Rebecca made no comment. The night before, she and Jared had worked until one a.m. gathering as much information as they could about Daryl Hawley and his wife.

Once they figured out Hawley's distinct use of hieroglyphics to differentiate the websites he frequented, they found his "cheat sheet" of passwords to be a huge help to them to get into his email and finance sites with ease. They also found the PIN that unlocked his phone. But the information gave them no discernible leads.

Again that morning, just as the day before, Rebecca's first activity was to phone the inspector in charge of finding the children. Cheryl Wong was already in the field. They were following every lead, no matter how slight, and working the neighborhood, including parks and any other "attractive" places for children to go. Counting from the time of Daryl Hawley's Sunday night death, the children had been missing some sixty hours. Cheryl, thank God, had released photos of the children to the media the previous day.

"Isn't it time to call in the FBI?" Rebecca asked.

"I'm afraid so." Cheryl paused a moment. "They like us to wait seventy-two hours but who's counting? The problem with the Feds is that once they step in we have to take orders from them."

"I've got an FBI contact who's somewhat reasonable," Rebecca said. "If that might help, just let me know."

While Rebecca was on the phone, she watched her fellow detectives arrive at work—Paavo Smith, Toshiro "Yosh" Yoshi-wara, Bo Benson, and Luis Calderon. They had all heard about Bill Sutter's sudden trial retirement and Jared Woolridge's detail to the bureau.

Each one greeted Woolridge, introduced himself, and tried to make him feel welcome. They didn't pump him with questions although it was obvious to Rebecca that they were filled with curiosity.

Once Rebecca was off the phone, they looked to her for answers, but with Jared sitting right there, all she could do was to speak in platitudes. She let them know she had talked with Sutter and that he was doing "okay." Her carefully chosen words told them there was more to the story, but nothing she could discuss at the moment. They nodded and kept their questions to themselves, at least for the time being.

Medical examiner Dr. Evelyn Ramirez called Rebecca with the verbal results of the Daryl Hawley autopsy. A written report would soon follow. She confirmed the cause of death as a bullet to the back of the head. Hawley had a little alcohol but no drugs in his system when he was killed.

For the second day in a row, per Richie's instructions, Vito Grazioso headed for the mayor's home in his wife's compact Mazda.

Yesterday's surveillance had been so dull tracking the mayor from his home to City Hall to a golf course and then the same stops in reverse, Vito wasn't looking forward to the day's adventure.

After watching the mayor's private residence for over an hour and seeing no one visit, Vito was glad when Cornelius Warren left home.

Vito followed, hoping the mayor might do something more interesting than he had the day before, but his heart sank when Warren's driver took him to City Hall. Vito had a strong sense of déjà vu as he pulled out his City Hall parking pass.

He was only there twenty minutes, however, when Deputy Mayor Dianne Cahill strode across the garage to her car, a gray Tesla. Vito sat up and took notice, not only because she was easy on the eyes.

Why, he wondered, would she be leaving her office so early in the morning? And alone? If there was a political reason such as a speech or a ribbon-cutting ceremony, she would have an entourage with her. But she didn't.

It could be nothing, he told himself. A dental appointment

maybe. Yet, something seemed off. Even the way she looked over her shoulder as if to see if anyone was watching, gave Vito pause.

He went with instinct, and when the deputy mayor left the parking garage, he followed.

Before he knew it, she had led him to one of the poorest sectors of the city.

But then he turned a corner, and no longer saw her car.

How in the ...?

He circled the block, and only after a careful perusal did he realize what had happened.

Dianne Cahill had turned into a driveway that led to the back lot of a small building just off Balou Street. He could barely make out the washed out lettering on the front of the building: Ventura Bros Mortuary.

Vito parked the Mazda a few doors away and waited, his camera ready.

Before long, a Lexus approached. He took as many photos of the car, its license plate, and windows as he could, hoping at least one photo would give him a good view of the driver. All he could tell was that the driver was male.

Interesting, he thought, as the many stories about Madame Deputy's love life came back to him. For many years, she had been seen dancing and dining with the cream of San Francisco society, which meant not only old money but also new, with much of it centered on Google and Oracle. The Twitter guys tended to be too young for her.

For the past few years, however, pictures of her had all but vanished from the society page. Word was that she had found love, but instead of someone wealthy, the man who stole her heart apparently had little money or anything else to offer her.

There were rumors that she didn't want anyone to see him with her because he was an underling who worked for the city.

Such a liaison could lead to a sticky personnel situation if she wanted to help advance his career.

No one knew who the mystery man was. Vito wondered if the pictures he took might hold the answer, although some poor church mouse of an employee was likely not driving a Lexus. And he couldn't imagine the back lot of a mortuary as a trysting spot for anyone.

Although, as the great Italian poet, Dante Alighieri, wrote (after reading Dante's *Divine Comedy*, Vito decided he didn't need to bother with any other book and kept re-reading that one), "Love insists the loved loves back."

Maybe, Vito thought, this was the only place they dared openly show their love. But then, as Vito contemplated the difficulties of morganatic relationships, another car arrived.

This one was an Audi, driven by a woman.

Scratch the love theme, Vito thought, as he again took photos. He felt bad about that. Much as he hated to admit it, Vito had a romantic soul, and he often thought Dianne Cahill was a nice person who should find someone to share, intimately, the riches of her life. He couldn't imagine what a disaster his life would be without his wife Florence and their children. He had to admit that Florence ruled their household with an iron fist, but over the iron she had the good sense to wear a velvet glove.

The meeting, to Vito's surprise, lasted fifteen minutes before the deputy's Tesla, the Audi, and the Lexus all left the mortuary lot. Vito couldn't help but think those three cars were worth more than all the buildings on this block combined—the buildings, not the land they sat on.

Vito was good at reading people and the way each driver looked up and down the street told him they were guilty of something. He slumped down in the car seat as the autos drove away.

He was pleased to come up with another of his favorite Dante quotes: "Midway on our life's journey, I found myself in dark woods, the right road lost." He couldn't help but think those wealthy people must have taken a very wrong road indeed to end up having secret meetings in an area like this.

Now, he just had to find out where that road was leading them.

When Vito returned to City Hall, the mayor's car was no longer in its parking space.

Richie was gonna be pissed.

14

S hay made himself a cup of tea, then opened the morning *San Francisco Chronicle*.

The above-the-fold story had to do with two children that had gone missing after the murder of their father. A shudder went through him at the thought of a missing or kidnapped child. Such a story had more meaning to him than ever before. He noticed that Rebecca had the lead in the murder investigation. There was a photo of the distraught mother. He hoped the children would be found safe and sound sometime soon, and quickly turned the page away from the upsetting story.

In the past, he rarely bothered to give the paper more than a passing glance since local news didn't interest him. Most days he hadn't bothered to look at it at all.

Studying local news had become one of many changes in his life over the past three weeks. Not that he had grown interested in most of it—in fact, he hated reading it. But he needed to for a particular reason: the murder case against Hannah's mother, the woman who was the love of his life, Salma Najjar.

Unfortunately, Rebecca Mayfield was the homicide inspector on the case. She wasn't one to give up looking for and arresting

Salma, despite knowing about Salma's relationship with Shay and that she was Hannah's mother.

Rebecca still believed in justice and the legal system. Shay didn't, and that, he felt, was the sticking point between them.

After much thought, he decided the best way to handle the situation was to convince Rebecca that Salma was dead so she would close the investigation. To do that, after Salma was safely out of the country, he removed her car from his garage and drove it to a restricted parking area near Ocean Beach. On the passenger seat he had placed a suicide note addressed to Homicide Inspector Rebecca Mayfield.

He'd expected that after a few days someone would notice an abandoned car and call for the city to tow it away. Then the note would be found, and the police called. But the day before he had driven out to the beach to find the car was still there collecting parking tickets.

The whole thing was no end of frustrating. All he could do was to continue to wait for someone to find the suicide note, and for the news of its discovery to break.

His problem was his daughter. She was a bright child. At eight years old, she could read the newspaper and sometimes she even watched the news on television.

When she first came to live with him, stories about Salma and the two murders she had allegedly committed were all over the news. Somehow Shay had kept Hannah away from all newspapers and all local television stations. After about a week of nothing new happening, and Salma's whereabouts remaining unknown, the media moved on to other stories.

Shay was sure that once word hit about finding Salma's car and a suicide note, media interest would again erupt. He knew he couldn't shield such news from Hannah forever, and that he would need to support her once the story broke.

He, who had never been around children for any length of

time, now had to deal with his own child hearing that her mother had done horrible things and had taken her own life—and all the while knowing it was a lie. He wasn't sure how to handle it.

He picked up the newspaper and inspected each article in it.

Again, this day, he could breathe a sigh of mixed relief. The story wasn't in the paper. Yet.

Rebecca was tired of excuses. She had phoned Tracy Hawley several times, but her sister, Pam, always answered. Pam was worse than some centurion protecting a Roman emperor with one excuse after the other. "Tracy is too upset to talk to you." "The sleeping pill Tracy took is too strong for her to answer questions." "Tracy's doctor says she needs complete rest and quiet."

Bull crap.

Rebecca and Jared headed to Tracy's apartment.

Normally, the spouse is the first person detectives look at when there's a murder, particularly one that takes place in a victim's house. In this case, with the missing children, Rebecca really didn't think Tracy was involved. But for two days she'd been blocked from questioning the woman, and the longer this kept on, the greater her suspicions became.

The apartment building was on Ulloa and 25th Avenue. It was a nice middle class area, considerably better than the neighborhood Daryl Hawley lived in. Rebecca rang the bell and was buzzed inside.

Pam stood at the door scowling fiercely as Rebecca and Jared climbed the stairs to the second floor. Pam stood aside and let them enter without a word.

The living room was tiny, with a sectional sofa taking up most of the floor space. In front of it was an equally large coffee table and everything faced the television. The coffee table had used coffee cups and plates on it, and Pam quickly picked them up.

"We need to see Tracy," Rebecca said leaving no room for argument.

Anger flared in Pam's eyes before she turned and left the room.

Rebecca and Jared sat. "We'll give her one minute," Rebecca said, her mouth a firm line.

The minute was almost up when Tracy Hawley approached. Except that she was wearing a bathrobe, no makeup, and hadn't combed her hair, she didn't look very different from the weepy yet belligerent woman Rebecca had encountered Monday morning.

The two inspectors stood. "Hello, Tracy," Rebecca said. "This is my new partner, Jar—"

"I don't give a shit," Tracy said. The way she slurred her words, the way she tottered as she faced them, it was clear she'd been drinking. "Have you found my kids yet?"

"Jared Woolridge," Rebecca finished. "We're working on Daryl's murder. I'm sure the SVU has been in touch with you about Molly and Porter."

"Fat lot of good they're doing. Bunch of B.S. And now they're questioning me! *Are they fucking crazy?* I didn't kidnap my own kids, for cryin' out loud! What the hell are they thinking? I can't take it anymore! I really can't!"

"Tracy," Rebecca's voice was low and calm. "We need to ask you some questions. There's a good possibility that whoever killed Daryl has your children. If you can help us find Daryl's killer, we might find the kids as well."

Tracy shook her head. "No! That can't be. If they saw who killed Daryl, they'll be killed. You know it. So I will *not* listen to you say such a thing."

"Mrs. Hawley," Jared said, his voice soothing. "We want to

find your little ones. Forget SVU. We'll find them for you, but you need to answer some of our questions. Please, Tracy."

She looked up at him and her bottom lip trembled. "I'm so scared," she whispered, lifting her hands as if imploring him to help.

He took her hands in his. "I know you are. I can't imagine what you're going through. It's changed everything, hasn't it? Your job. Your friends. You probably question everything and everyone you've ever known."

She nodded. "It's true. Who would do this?"

He walked her to the sofa and sat beside her. Rebecca took the shorter part of the sectional, facing them. "Tell me about your job," Jared said.

"My job?" Tracy looked confused.

"You mentioned you work at a place called Blaxor. What is it?"

She pressed the bridge of her nose between her eyes before she spoke. "It's a pharmaceutical company." Then she gave a small chuckle. "Hell, I'm taking one of their products right now. Lulz. It's for anxiety."

"What do you do there?"

"I'm a manager in the billing department."

"Have you had the job very long?"

"Twelve years."

"Before you were married?" he asked.

She nodded. "I met Daryl at work. He was a stock boy. Very sweet. Sincere. I fell in love. Or thought I had." She shook her head. "What can I say? I was stupid."

"What caused your separation?"

"Look at where we were living. I helped Daryl get his job at RX Wholesale. He needed to do more than be a stock boy all his life. But he had no ambition. No wish to better himself. Not only would he gladly do nothing but drive that truck around all day, he didn't even want to move from that dump he called a house. It was close to his work, and that's all that mattered to him. I was so sick of it, I left."

"You could afford to be on your own?" Rebecca asked.

"Barely! A while back, I'd gotten a nice bonus at work and a promotion. I used the extra money to put our kids in private schools. And I kept saving. Finally, I had enough money saved to walk out. I'd hoped my leaving would cause Daryl to get off his ass and do something with his life. But he accepted that I had gone and still did nothing. And now he's dead."

"Do you have any idea who might have wanted him dead?" Jared asked. He glanced at Rebecca who was watching this tête-à-tête with her eyebrows half-way to her hairline. She nodded to him to keep going.

"None at all. I mean, he was hardly the type to make waves. Hell, he never even made a ripple."

Rebecca and Jared quizzed both Tracy and Pam thoroughly for the names of any friends, relatives, and acquaintances that might have some idea of what had made Daryl Hawley a target. The two women came up with no one.

"Can you think of anything at all that might have caused someone to become upset with him, or threaten him?" Jared asked for the umpteenth time.

Tracy clasped her hands together tight, then sucked in her breath and drew herself up to look squarely at Jared. "How many times do I have to tell you? He did nothing. Nothing. That's what he was all about. A big, fat zero. Now, instead of wasting time with these goddamned questions, will you please go out and *find my kids!*"

bout noon, Shay received a call from Vito.

"I've emailed some photos to you," Vito said. "This morning, on a hunch, I followed the Deputy Mayor. She met with a man and woman who look like they must have money. I caught it all."

A politician meeting people who have money was hardly anything to care about, Shay thought. "Why was this meeting of interest?"

"For one very good reason," Vito paused dramatically before continuing. "They held it in the back of a mortuary, now closed, out in the Bayview-Hunters Point area."

Shay's eyebrows rose. "That is interesting."

"And it continued for over fifteen minutes."

"You're right. It's worth looking into."

"Like I said," Vito added. Shay could hear the smile in his voice.

"Where are you now?" Shay asked.

"Outside a restaurant. The mayor, the deputy, and his chief of staff are inside having lunch with some lobbyists. It's all I can do to stay awake."

"Take care, and thanks," Shay said.

Shay went to his computer to view the photos. He could recognize Deputy Mayor Cahill, but the other drivers' features were fuzzy and distorted by their windshields and the angles of the photos. The license numbers of all three cars were clear.

Shay hacked into the California Department of Motor Vehicles database. He ran the first license. Varg Hague of San Francisco was listed as the owner. He then ran the second and learned someone named Paula Forsyth, also a resident of the city, owned the car.

He frowned. That was way too easy.

The Tesla driven by Dianne Cahill was on lease to the City and County of San Francisco. He rolled his eyes. Of course it was. Why should she pay for a car when the taxpayers could?

Shay had recently purchased a facial recognition system from a colleague who did business in China, so he used his new program to match the photos to the DMV's database of driver's license pictures. The program took only a little over three minutes to find five possible matches for the man, and seven for the woman.

"Well, look at that," he murmured. The names Varg Hague and Paula Forsyth were on the list.

He spent the rest of the afternoon doing research and then phoned Richie.

Back at her desk in Homicide, Rebecca made another call to Cheryl Wong. She knew she was being a pain, but she didn't care. Wong told her she had brought the FBI into the case but they, too, were having no luck locating the children.

Jared had returned to the crime scene to knock on doors to talk to more neighbors about Daryl and Tracy Hawley and ask if anyone had seen the Hawley children as well as any strangers in the neighborhood around the time Rebecca was shot at. He was able to give at least a partial description of the one man Rebecca had glimpsed.

Rebecca next began to work through all the names and numbers on Daryl's phone—calls and texts both made and received. Most incoming were spam, and the outgoing were to his boss or his wife. It seemed to be a rather dull life.

Rebecca had been fighting the feeling she should go out there and look for the children herself. But what could she do that a whole unit dedicated to finding missing or kidnapped children could not? And Jared was doing a lot of legwork out there as well.

But so far nothing in this case was adding up.

She sat back and tried to think this through. She and Jared had dashed about doing all the usual things in a homicide investigation—checking for odd fingerprints and any sign of a break-in at the residence. Nothing. Canvassing neighbors, interviewing family and co-workers for any hint of what might have caused troubles. Nothing. Looked at finances: too many bills, too little income, but other than that, nothing.

Somebody had coldly executed Daryl Hawley. Wives who killed their husbands usually did so in a fit of rage and struck them somewhere in the head or chest, not in the back of the head like a gangland assassin.

Rebecca was trying to determine what she and Jared were missing, and where they should go to find it.

She was going through interview write-ups, hoping she might have overlooked something, some minuscule nugget that could crack the case wide open, when Elizabeth buzzed her. "Someone is here to see you," the administrative assistant said. "You should come into the office now."

"Who is it?" Rebecca asked. But Elizabeth had already hung up.

Puzzled, Rebecca headed for the office. When she reached the doorway, she stopped, gawking in stunned disbelief at the person seated on a chair across the room.

"Look who's here!" Elizabeth sang out, beaming and gesturing toward the older woman.

"Mom!" Rebecca gasped, entering the office. "What in the world are you doing here?"

Lorene Mayfield straightened and then slowly stood. She didn't step toward her daughter in greeting, but remained where she was, clutching her handbag with both hands. She was in her early sixties with short, dyed blonde hair with frosted tips. She wore more eye makeup than Rebecca remembered her using, and a pinkish blush powder covered her cheeks. Her body showed only the slightest extra weight that often came with age, and she wore a stylish pale blue business suit and striped blouse. Rebecca thought she looked fit and healthy.

As Elizabeth eyed the expressions on each woman's face, her smile vanished. She quickly sat back down.

"Is that a way to greet me?" Lorene's voice was frosty. "I decided if you wouldn't come to Idaho to visit me, the least I could do is come here to see you."

"But…" Rebecca searched for words that Lorene couldn't take as confrontational. "How did you get here? Did you fly down?"

"I drove. I stayed overnight in Reno, and came away with an extra two hundred dollars off the slot machines." Lorene's chin rose. "Luck was with me."

"But to come all this way, without even telling me…. Is something wrong? You aren't sick are you?"

Lorene glanced over at the administrative assistant who was taking all of this in with great interest. "Of course not! Why shouldn't everything be just fine?"

Rebecca's gaze followed Lorene's. Elizabeth immediately

began staring at a slip of paper in front of her. This wasn't the best place for Rebecca and her mother to be conversing. "Let me get my things and we can go to my apartment," Rebecca said. "Do you have a place to stay?"

Lorene's lips pursed. "I didn't think I needed to find a hotel room when my daughter lives in the city."

"You're right," Rebecca acknowledged. "Whatever was I thinking?"

Richie lived in one of the nicest neighborhoods in San Francisco, high up on Twin Peaks near the center of the city. When the area wasn't fogged in—and it often was—he had a great view stretching from the city to the bay and the hills of Oakland and the East Bay beyond. Shay drove there with copies of the photos Vito took and the documents he'd gathered about the people in the photos.

As he arrived, Richie was getting ready to meet his newest client, the former antique dealer, William Roland Allen, but he always had time for Shay's findings.

"I guess Vito told you about the strange meeting Deputy Mayor Dianne Cahill had," Shay began after Richie got them both a beer. They sat in the living room.

"He did. In the back of a mortuary." Richie shook his head. "I wonder if there was some significance to that choice."

"If so, it's nothing good. With the car license plates, I found the drivers." He pointed to each as he spoke their names. "Paula Forsyth and Varg Hague. I also double-checked their photos off the DMV database. Here they are." Shay spread the photos on the coffee table, both the DMV and the ones Vito took.

Richie nodded, mentally filing away the names.

"I then ran those names against the California Franchise Tax

Board files to see where they worked and their income levels. Both work for Blaxor Pharmaceuticals in South San Francisco. Paula Forsyth's income was over three-hundred grand, and Hague's was half a million."

"Blaxor?" Richie said. "Never heard of them."

"Varg Hague is president, Forsyth first vice president. From what I could tell, three years ago Hague bought a struggling company, Blaxor, based on the promises of a break-out anti-anxiety drug, dialulzopan. He was hoping to sell it to Merck or some other Big Pharma company and make a fortune."

"He has a background in that?" Richie asked.

"Not at all," Shay said. "He's from Norway. Moved here with his wife for business opportunities. Met Paula Forsyth. She knows quite a few people in this area. She went to top schools, has an MBA, rose through the ranks of several corporations, and ended up at Blaxor. Hague is now divorced, Forsyth married, and both are in their mid-forties."

"So why would these two be meeting with Dianne Cahill?" Richie mused, trying to put these pieces together.

"That's where it gets interesting," Shay said. "I delved into Blaxor. Its best-selling drug is the one that caused Hague to buy the company. It now goes by the brand name Lulz, as in 'it lulls you into a carefree existence.' And guess who its biggest purchaser is?"

Richie frowned. "If Dianne Cahill is involved, it must be the city of San Francisco."

"You got it in one," Shay said with a smile.

"Why? What are they using it for? I know politicians love their drugs, but to be the biggest purchaser …"

Shay leaned back in his chair and smiled. It had taken him a while, but he'd worked it out. "As far as I can tell, shortly after Hague bought Blaxor, the city began supplying its free health clinics with Lulz for its hardline homeless population. The main benefit of Lulz was that when a person stopped taking it they suffered few dangerous side-effects. That was a good thing when dealing with a population known to have difficulty sticking to a regimen of pill-taking."

"Okay," Richie said, clearly uninterested in the history.

"But there was a problem," Shay added. "About two-and-a-half years ago, an FDA review of Lulz showed that its benefits were negligible. It did no harm, but it also seemed to do little good. And that, apparently, is why people who go off it suffer few side effects. The term 'placebo' comes to mind. A very expensive placebo, too, since there's no generic equivalent."

"And that must be why Hague still owns the company," Richie said., realizing the FDA study effectively killed Lulz as a takeover target.

Shay nodded. "True, but then, two months ago, purchases of Lulz by the city jumped tenfold."

Richie grimaced. "There's only one reason for the city to buy a drug that does little good and costs a lot of money. Someone has to be growing rich off it. And, based on Vito's surveillance, we have a good idea of who."

The top of Nob Hill is an exclusive area surrounded by Grace Cathedral, entrances to the Fairmont and Mark Hopkins hotels, the Pacific Union Club, and the Masonic Auditorium.

Although Rebecca lived near it, her apartment was in Mulford Alley on the southern, downside of the hill toward the area known as the Tenderloin. Since the earliest days of San Francisco, the area was known for prostitution and drugs. Its name came about when someone said the only cops who could afford to buy expensive Tenderloin cuts of beef worked there—although whether the extra money came from hazardous-duty pay or bribes was a matter of dispute.

The best thing about living in Mulford Alley was that the curb on one side of the street was painted red, making it a "no parking" zone. But since meter maids never entered the alley, those who lived there soon discovered they could park with impunity.

Now, Rebecca drove over the curb, up onto the red-painted sidewalk, and shut off the engine. Her mother followed in her Subaru Outback, but left her engine running.

Rebecca got out and hurried to her mother. "Here we are."

"What is this place?" Lorene asked sharply as she rolled down her window.

"This is where I live."

"It looks like an alley."

"It is. Let's get your suitcase and go inside."

"But I'm illegally parked."

"So am I."

Lorene's eyes narrowed. "We're not going to leave our cars up on the sidewalk, are we?"

"We are."

Lorene sucked in her breath and followed Rebecca. Her next shock was when Rebecca, rather than going to the main entrance to the building, walked to a grim, in-need-of-paint door that stood beside the garage doors. Rebecca unlocked the door and pushed it open.

As Lorene peered into the darkness her expression went from worried to horrified. "What in the world is this?" she asked. "You live in there? Is it safe?"

"Absolutely." Rebecca stepped through the doorway and waited. Lorene hesitantly followed. "This is the breezeway to the backyard and my apartment. It's a very nice little place."

Lorene's eyes were large and round as she waited for Rebecca to lock the door behind them.

They soon reached a small cement-covered backyard that received little sunlight. In the center stood a large planter box filled with shade-loving greenery, a few flowers, and some herbs. Rebecca noticed Lorene's face tighten at the tiny space. Rebecca, however, always considered this bit of outdoors in the heart of the city as one of the best parts of her home.

She continued to her front door. As soon as she opened it, Spike burst out, barked at Lorene and then jumped up and down until Rebecca picked up his wriggling little body and gave him a hug and a kiss on the top of his head. She then put him down so he could run over to the sandy corner of the yard which had become his designated potty area.

"Oh my Lord," Lorene gasped. "Is that a dog? What in the world happened to its fur? And why does it have those big pink and brown's spots all over its body?"

"That's the breed, a Chinese crested—it's hairless. I think he's cute." Rebecca couldn't hide the indignant tone of her voice.

"Cute?" Lorene looked at her daughter as if she'd lost her mind. "That's the ugliest dog I've ever seen!"

As if he understood, Spike trotted over to Lorene, bared his teeth and growled. Lorene took a step back.

Rebecca picked him up and entered the apartment. "Let's go inside. He'll get used to you and stop growling. Eventually. He's my protector," she said, hugging and trying to calm the little fellow. "It's okay, guy. She's just my mother."

She suspected Spike was picking up her anxiety at having Lorene there. Dogs were good that way, and she had a lot of tension for Spike to sense. Rebecca and her mother never saw eye-to-eye about much at all. And to make matters worse, whenever critical words came out of Lorene's mouth, Rebecca's first tendency was to argue. One argument usually led to another, and nothing was ever resolved. That was a big reason Rebecca had stopped going back to Idaho.

She and her mother talked on the phone once every month or two, and always on birthdays and major holidays. But neither ever called just to say, "Hi, how are you? I miss you and want to talk." They didn't have that kind of relationship.

Rebecca led her mother to the bedroom. "You can sleep in here. I'll take the sofa," she said. "My hours are strange, and that'll be most convenient."

Lorene was aghast at the postage-stamp size apartment. She nodded, then sat on the bed, looking a little dazed.

~

Soon after Shay finished explaining all he'd found about the meeting between the deputy mayor and the bigwigs at Blaxor, he left the house. Richie felt good about Shay and Vito's findings. It was a better start than he imagined they'd come up with, and it had happened much more quickly than expected. Thank God for Vito's intuition about shady people.

Richie probably should have asked them to look into William Roland Allen. Richie hadn't yet found much of anything about the guy. He'd briefly mentioned his meeting to Shay, telling him William Roland Allen sounded like a character out of a spy novel, then laughed it off. There was something fishy about the guy, but that was something Richie could handle on his own.

At the moment, he was more interested in whether or not Willie—as he'd come to think of his would-be client—would come up with the money Richie required to investigate his black-mail situation. Richie never could find out much about the guy. At the moment, he was more interested in whether or not Willie—as he'd come to think of his client—would come up with the money Richie wanted. If not, having Vito or Shay look into the man's background would have been a waste of their time. Time much better spent dealing with Rebecca's problem.

Willie asked to meet at a small bar in the Marina district near the corner of Chestnut and Scott. Richie always liked the Marina, a pretty area of small but expensive homes near the north bay. Richie was driving around the block, looking for parking when he got a phone call from a friend, Sam Giovanni, who was a patrolman in Central Station. He pushed the button for hands-free conversation.

"Sam, how you doing?"

"Not bad. But I just heard something I think will interest you."

"Oh?"

"Your friend in homicide, did you know someone took a shot at her yesterday while she was checking out a crime scene?"

"What?" Richie was stunned. *"Yesterday?"*

"That's right. Sounds like she kept it from you, buddy. I kind of figured that. Word is, it was suspicious. Didn't make a lot of sense. Almost as if she was specifically targeted."

"Christ almighty," Richie murmured. Why in the hell hadn't she told him about it? "Thanks, Sam," Richie said. "I owe you one."

"No problem."

By the time the call ended, Richie was beyond steamed. He tried to phone Rebecca, but she wasn't answering. Damn! Why would she keep something like that a secret? What was wrong with her? Did she have a death wish?

He continued to drive around looking for parking, squelching the desire to find her and try to force some sense into her. This was no game, damn it.

He noticed a small space on Avila. He squeezed into it, all the while clenching his jaw so hard it ached. He could only hope meeting Willie-boy would calm him down a little before he caught up with Rebecca.

Earlier, he had noticed a black SUV circling the same area as he was, probably also looking for a parking place. As he got out of the Porsche, he gave it a pat, grateful for its small size.

Moments later, the black SUV turned onto Avila. His mind fuming over Rebecca, he didn't think much of it until it drew near and he saw what looked like the barrel of a handgun being held outside the window. Blue-black tattoos speckled the arm holding the gun.

At the same moment, Shay's Maserati appeared at the other end of the block. Shay gunned his engine and roared toward the

SUV, one hand on the steering wheel, the other on his monster Sig Sauer P226, also sticking out of the window.

"What the hell?" Richie dived behind his Porsche. No good could come of being between those two behemoths.

The SUV howled as the brakes were slammed on, and it then began a lurching weave backwards down the street, sideswiping a couple of cars as it went. Shay stopped when he reached Richie. "Get in," he called.

Richie leapt in, and Shay sped toward the end of the block where the SUV had turned. They saw it ahead of them, racing toward the expressway that led to the Golden Gate Bridge.

"We could catch up to it eventually," Shay said. "What do you say?"

"Forget it. They're nothing. Probably just some muscle paid to get rid of me. Just like Willie-the-antique-swindler was probably just some paid actor. He was phony, but I thought it was an act to get me to take the case."

"Instead," Shay said, "it was an act to get you. Period."

"How did you figure it out?" Richie asked.

"I didn't feel comfortable with what you told me about your would-be client. The whole thing smelled, and something told me your meeting was a setup, and I figured it was a good idea for me to be nearby if anything went wrong."

As much as he hated to think it, a lot of things were going wrong and there was no doubt in his mind that Rebecca was being set-up, too.

Since the police would descend on the area Shay and Richie were in because of the side-swiped parked cars, Richie would have to wait a few hours before picking up his Porsche.

He told Shay he'd just learned Rebecca had been in a

shootout the day before. It confirmed both men's sense that the latest thwarted attack on Richie could well be part of some master plan against them. More than anything, Richie wanted to see Rebecca, face-to-face, right then. He had Shay drive him to her apartment.

When they reached Mulford Alley, Richie was relieved to see Rebecca's SUV parked in its usual place. Since she was home, he got out of the car and Shay left.

He used the keys she'd given him to let himself past the breezeway door. Once he reached her apartment, however, he always knocked. That, he thought, seemed only polite.

Almost immediately, Rebecca opened the door. She wore a strange expression and, instead of inviting him in, she stepped outside.

As much as he wanted to show her how angry he was at her for not telling him about being shot at, he couldn't. She was safe; he was safe. Thank you, Lord … and Shay.

He put his arms around her and kissed her. But instead of leaning into his kiss the way she usually did, she stepped back.

He studied her face. "You have something you want to tell me, don't you?"

She looked surprised. "You've already heard?"

"I have."

She drew in her breath. "In that case, you may as well come inside."

He nodded, imagining they would sit down and she would tell him all about the shootout she had been involved in.

But he took only one step into her apartment when he froze at the sight of an older woman glaring at him. She was tall and blond, with blue eyes, a pointy chin … and looked like she took no prisoners. He understood. "You must be Rebecca's mother," he said with a smile as he walked toward her, his hand extended. "I've heard so many nice things about you."

"You have?" Lorene barely touched the hand he offered as she glanced from him to Rebecca and back.

Yes, he'd heard quite a bit about her from Rebecca. Warnings, mostly. But this ice queen treatment was even more than he had imagined. "Welcome to San Francisco." Normally, he'd hug a person who was a relative of someone he was close to, but the way she was standing, he feared she might crack and dissolve into dust.

Some inner demon made him add, "I see where Rebecca gets her good looks."

"Oh?" Lorene's eyes again met Rebecca's, looking completely confused.

Rebecca stepped between them. "This is Richard Amalfi. He's the fellow Courtney told you about."

That caused Richie to give her a double-take. Courtney told her mother about him? Rebecca's sister had met Richie on a recent visit to the city.

"I see." Lorene's lips scarcely moved as she spoke. She sat down on the edge of the sofa, her hands primly folded on her lap, and regarded Richie warily. The Queen of England couldn't sit more stiffly or look more arch.

He took the rocking chair, head cocked as he studied Rebecca who appeared more agitated with each passing second.

She fled to the kitchen area. "Wine anyone? Coffee? Tea?"

"Coffee," Lorene said.

"Same," Richie murmured.

Rebecca poured a glass of Cabernet Sauvignon for herself. A full one.

Richie's eyebrows went up the slightest bit but then he put an ingratiating smile on his face and turned to Lorene. "I've wanted to meet you for the longest time. I'm glad to finally do so."

She gave him a pert nod. "How interesting to hear Rebecca talked about me to you. It's too bad she didn't return the favor."

He gave a quick glance toward Rebecca who was now making coffee. "I know what you mean," he said. "She's one of the most difficult people I've ever come across to get to talk about herself, or what she's been up to, or what she's doing. It's as if her life is some national secret and you need to join the CIA to find out anything. At least, that's the way she is around me," Richie said. "Maybe you have more luck. If so, I wish you'd tell me the secret."

Lorene nodded in agreement even as her lips remained frozen in a tight grimace.

Rebecca brought out the coffee and gave a cup to Richie. "Mom just arrived. Unexpectedly. And she'll stay with me a few days. Isn't that nice?" Her voice had taken on a fake girlish lilt. Rebecca never "lilted."

"A few days. I see." He gave her a look that told her exactly how 'nice' he thought it was, but then he faced Lorene. "That's great. Is there any special reason for you to be here, or is it for fun and seeing Rebecca?"

"The latter," Lorene said as Rebecca handed her mother a cup.

"Are you staying here?" Richie asked Lorene.

"That's the idea," Lorene said. "I didn't get a hotel room. Do you know what a decent hotel costs in this city? It's outrageous!"

"That's true, but this will be cozy," Richie said with a look of commiseration on his face. "It's hardly big enough for one, let alone two."

Lorene seemed to appreciate his recognition of the suffering she was about to undertake. "So I've noticed."

"We'll be fine," Rebecca chimed in, then gulped some wine.

"Do you two have any plans yet for dinner?" he asked.

"No," Rebecca said. "I'll pick up a few things at the deli. Then, I need to go back to Homicide. We still haven't found the kids."

Richie faced Lorene. "Do you like Italian food, Mrs. Mayfield?"

"I like pizza as long as it's not too spicy. Hawaiian is my favorite. And my church group holds a spaghetti feed from time to time, but I don't much care for tomato sauce."

"Nice." Richie could scarcely get the word out. Everything she said he considered an affront to his ancestral palate. "How about I take you both to dinner tonight? I'll have to work at it, but I might be able to top a group feed."

Lorene then announced she'd had a miserable day so far driving on the wretchedly crowded California freeways and the even worse traffic in San Francisco, and she needed to lie down for a few minutes before going anywhere. She picked up her coffee and went off to the bedroom.

Rebecca and Richie took Spike and went out to the backyard.

"She is something," Richie said as he and Rebecca sat on a bench.

"The poster child for 'hell on wheels,'" Rebecca said. She looked miserable.

"Tell me what's going on?" He draped an arm over her shoulders.

"I have no idea." She leaned against him. "She just showed up in Homicide. She was the last thing I was expecting, and I don't know why she's here. I can't imagine she'll be here long."

"I'm not talking about your mother. I'm talking about someone shooting at you yesterday. Who was it? What happened? *And why the hell didn't you tell me about it?*"

She sat up straight. "Because there was nothing to tell. Someone was lurking in the yard of my crime scene. I went after him, he and a friend shot back. They missed. My new partner and I searched, but they were long gone. It could have been anyone. It's a high-crime area. They might have been kids hoping to steal something in a house where the only resident is now dead. I have no idea."

He scowled. "That was a nice speech. How long did you practice it?"

"Richie—"

He stopped her excuses by telling her about his faux client, and how Shay probably saved his life—and not for the first time.

The coloring had all but vanished from Rebecca's cheeks when he finished. "Who is that person? Why are you a target? It's not because of what's going on with me, is it? Tell me you aren't in danger because of my job."

"It's not only because of you. These are powerful people, and they know I would love to see them all in prison, or worse. They also know that if they did anything to hurt you, I won't stop until they pay—and, I expect, you feel the same way."

"I do." She ran her hand along the side of his face. "I can't bear thinking of you in danger," she said, then put her arms around him.

"As long as you're safe, I'll be fine," he murmured as they kissed.

"All right," Lorene's voice rang out. "I'm ready to go to dinner now."

17

He opened the door to the basement. Immediately, he saw that the lights were on. *Clever little devils, aren't they?*

The children sat at the bottom of the stairs staring up at him.

He wondered how much they liked seeing walls black with mildew, empty coffins, and even a table filled with ancient embalming implements and a few glass jars with heaven only knew what strange things inside them. Most looked to him like malformed innards, tumors, or simply unknown body parts.

The only good thing down there were the pretty dolls he'd collected over the years. His only friends.

The dolls made no noise. He liked quiet. The two brats had cried and screamed so much the day before when he brought them cereal and milk—a kindness, he thought—that he gave serious thought to leaving them alone for a day or more. No food. No water. Then they might appreciate him.

But his better nature won out, and he had relented. He brought them a sack of hamburgers and fries.

"Do you know how to play checkers?" he called down to them.

In one hand was a battery-operated lantern, in the other, a checkers game. He put down the no-longer-needed lantern.

"Do you?" he asked again, only to be met with silence. "Play checkers?"

The children still didn't answer. He picked up the game and walked down the stairs. "I guess you don't."

This was the first time he had allowed them to see his face. He knew he wasn't much to look at. When he was young like these two, other kids taunted him about it. "Piggy face" they had called him. Only his sister never picked on him. She protected him. Just like Porter and Molly did each other. Soon, they'd like him the way his sister once did.

"You can eat while I explain the game to you." He sat on the floor and put down the sack of food and the game in front of him. "My name is Frederick, but you can call me Freddie."

Porter took Molly's hand, and the two backed away.

"Where are you going?" Freddie asked. "Sit down."

"We don't want to play any stupid game," Porter yelled. "We want to go home!"

"Stop whining! I'm sick of hearing it. Sit!"

"No!"

He picked up the game and stood. "Don't you realize nobody cares about you? They've all left you. I'm the only one who cares."

"My Mommy cares," Molly said defiantly.

"Not so much," he roared. "She's got a new boyfriend. She's much happier with him without you two underfoot."

"That's not true!" Porter cried. "And our daddy loves us. He'll find us."

"Your daddy is dead, you stupid little butterball. He's not going to find anything ever again."

"No! I don't believe you," Porter shouted.

"Me neither!" Molly added.

Freddie moved closer, grabbed Molly's little arm, and pulled her toward him. "If your mother wanted you, she would have found you by now. She could have called the police and they would have used their dogs to find you. But she hasn't even tried. She doesn't want you anymore!"

"No! I hate you!" Molly tried to pull her arm free, but couldn't. Porter grabbed her, trying to help, but Freddie pushed him down and away so hard he skidded along the filthy cement floor, scraping his arms and elbows.

Both kids were crying now.

Freddie tucked the game under his arm. "You two need to shut up! I can't play with crying kids. Tomorrow, I'll be back and you will learn checkers, or else." He thought a moment, then added, "If you can beat me at it, maybe I'll let you upstairs so you can see the sun again."

He chuckled at that, then reached out and gave Molly's pony-tail a hard yank. He softly sang "Rock-A-Bye Baby" as he climbed the stairs to leave.

Porter and Molly knew the words and noticed that Freddie looked back at them with a cold gleam in his eyes and sang the last verse even louder. "And down will come baby, cradle and all."

18

"It's good to see you again," Dianne Cahill said. Despite it being only seven-thirty in the morning, she looked as if she'd been busy at work for some time.

"Good to see you, as well," Jared said. That morning he'd gotten a call from Cahill's secretary saying the deputy mayor wanted to meet with him before he went to Homicide. He now sat in her office in City Hall. He had never been there before and had to admit to being more than a little stunned by the thick Persian carpet and black and gold Egyptian motif that the room's designer had used. It felt more like a room in a museum than an office. He had met the Deputy Mayor twice before at police functions, but never one-on-one.

"Don't look so worried." She smiled at him. "I'm just wondering how things are going in your new position."

He didn't believe that for a moment. "Fine," he said. "It's interesting work."

She folded her hands atop her desk. "You're wondering why I called you here, aren't you?"

"Well, yes," he admitted.

"I called you in to explain that there's more to your detail than you've been told." She eyed him closely.

He stiffened. "I thought there might be."

"First, let me assure you that Commissioner Barcelli and I believe you'll make a fine homicide inspector. I also know you've done some special work for the commissioner in the past. Believe me when I say he sang your praises as one of our most loyal officers. I fully expect to reward such loyalty and dedication in the future."

Jared nodded and sat taller in the chair. "Thank you."

She cocked her head. "What did the commissioner tell you about this assignment?"

"Not too much," he said. As she stared expectantly at him, he added, "Only that there are concerns about some of the homicide inspectors. And that there's need for new blood in the bureau. New ideas, perhaps."

Her lips pursed, then she gave a fake smile. "That sounds like him."

Jared swallowed hard, unsure what to say.

"Let me explain fully." She leaned toward him and lowered her voice a bit. "You worked closely with Internal Affairs in your last job, and we want something similar now. Bringing in anyone from Internal Affairs would have been too obvious. You are not."

He remained silent.

"Our concern is not 'some' inspectors, Jared, it's one in particular." Her large brown eyes captured his and held. "Rebecca Mayfield. Some things have happened in the past that have caused the department to question her loyalty."

He was stunned to hear that.

Cahill continued. "I've spoken to Commissioner Barcelli about this, and because of the sensitive nature of the situation, I want you to report directly to me anything she does that you feel is at all sketchy."

He swallowed hard at both her words and the intensity of her gaze. "Sketchy?" He wasn't sure how Cahill meant that word.

"She's been involved in a number of cases where both her judgement and her attitude have been more than a little suspect. She's being sued by a victim of her bigotry, or 'alleged' bigotry, named Virginia Kirk. Also, she's having an affair with someone the department doesn't trust. So far, we haven't been able to catch him in anything illegal, but we're sure it's just a matter of time."

Jared's head was already spinning from the charges hurled at Rebecca when Cahill handed him a folder. He opened it. "The first photo is Richard Amalfi. Other photos are some of the people Amalfi has been involved with in the past. You'll find many unsavory characters in it. A clean cop would have nothing to do with Amalfi or the crooks he hangs around with."

"You believe Rebecca isn't a clean cop?" He couldn't reconcile the charge with what he saw of her attitude and work ethic.

"That's precisely what I believe. But I need proof. That's where you come in. I want to know what she's planning to do each day, where she'll be, and who she'll be with. And if you see anything illegal, let me know immediately. Is all this clear?"

"Quite," he said.

Cahill gave him a significant gaze, and then said, "I know your background."

He blanched. "My what?"

"Commissioner Barcelli and I go way, way back. Back to when he was captain of the Southern Station, and you were one of his officers. Some real shit happened back then, and I know Barcelli saved you from not only dismissal, but from prison time. And we all know what happens to cops in prison."

Jared's jaw tightened. "The 'saving' went both ways, if I remember correctly. Instead of jail, he got a promotion."

She smiled. "Yes, you two were quite the pair. And I like your gumption at pointing all that out. Not, of course, that I'd forgotten any of it. We all have long memories around here, and know where all the bodies are buried."

"Okay." He drew in his breath. "I understand what you're saying."

"I knew you would." She walked around her desk toward him. He jumped to his feet, thinking the interview must be over. "Now, promise me you won't tell anyone about our conversation." She smiled up at him, a smile at once coyly girlish, but also alluring— even with a hint of promise. Maybe more than a hint.

She was always attractive, but up close she exuded more raw sensuality that he expected. Words escaped him.

She turned serious. "Keep this from Lieutenant Eastwood for now. I don't know how many other people she might have compromised over the past few years. I don't want to take any chances."

"Right." The word was a whisper.

"I knew I could count on you." she murmured.

He felt as if he'd turned into a pool of jelly at her feet. "Always."

"Fine," she said with a smile that seemed for him alone. "You can go now."

He hurried out of the office. Once in the hall, he felt the need to take a few deep breaths. He wasn't sure exactly what had happened in there, but he knew he was stuck, and that nothing good would come of it.

Mrs. Brannigan marched into the dining room where Shay sat with the *San Francisco Chronicle* in front of him, eating his usual breakfast of one hard-boiled egg, toast with lemon curd, and tea. The housekeeper clasped her hands. "Mr. Tate, I'm afraid Miss Hannah is very upset this morning."

He had been about to drink some tea. Instead, he lowered the cup and frowned. "She is? Why?"

"She won't tell me what's bothering her," Mrs. Brannigan said.

Shay's brow furrowed. "Is she still upset about those kids questioning her?"

"I doubt it, but she's not saying. She can be a stubborn little thing," Mrs. Brannigan folded her arms. "She reminds me of someone she's closely related to."

"I don't know that she'll talk to me, either," Shay admitted. He couldn't get over the sense that instead of growing closer to him, she seemed more remote with each passing day. He wouldn't admit that to Mrs. Brannigan, however.

The housekeeper's eyes turned sad. "I don't think it has to do with you, Mr. Tate, or her school. I suspect the problem is that the poor little thing misses her mother and her brother. They were the centers of her life and suddenly she finds herself living with a stranger who says he's her father, her mother has vanished, and she's unable to see her brother. Even the man she thought was her father, who apparently always treated her well, is no longer a part of her life. To tell the truth, I'm amazed she's handled all this as well as she has."

Shay heaved a heavy sigh. "You're right. I need to remember how hard all this would be on an adult, and she's only eight."

"I think she'll feel better if she has a long heart-to-heart with her father," Mrs. Brannigan said.

The words cut through Shay. "You don't mean Gebran Najjar—"

"I mean *you*! Mr. Tate, you are an interesting and handsome man, and I know the child is quite taken with the fact that you're her real father. She's old enough to understand about romantic love, and to recognize that her mother and Gebran did not have that kind of relationship, but that you and her mother did. And she's even hinted to me she loves knowing that. She recognized how very unhappy her mother was with Gebran. I expect she'll be more than willing to give you at least a hint of what's troubling her. You can't continue to ignore her."

"I don't ignore her," Shay insisted, indignant. "I might not have long conversations with her, or 'play days' and all that, but I speak to her. I mean, what do I know about talking to a child?"

"It's time you learned." The housekeeper abruptly turned and marched toward the kitchen.

"Wait!" Shay's voice was almost pleading. "You said she's upset. You know how to handle her. I don't."

Mrs. Brannigan responded with "the look." One eyebrow went up, her chin tucked in, and sharp eyes that stared at him as if to say that if she were his mother instead of his housekeeper, he'd be in big trouble. "You're her father. It's time you acted like it."

He felt insulted, ready to argue. But the feeling passed almost immediately. She was right. She usually was. That was why he put up with her bossing him when it should have been the other way around. She was the only person he knew who could make him feel guilty about not living up to her expectations.

"All right. I'll talk to her." He left his tea and toast unfinished, took a deep breath, and headed for Hannah's room.

He knocked.

"Come in." Her voice was tiny.

He walked into the bedroom. Once, it had been an elegant guest room with a high four-poster bed and antiques. But when Hannah moved in he had paid an interior decorator to quickly turn it into a room fit for a young princess. Shay realized too late he should have asked Hannah if the white furnishings with silver trim were to her liking. But he wasn't used to thinking about—or caring—what other people's tastes were.

She had seemed pleased when she saw the change in the room. For one thing, she didn't have to fear breaking a bone if she fell out of bed. This one was much more her size.

He didn't go into her room often, but usually stopped at the doorway to tell her things like, "it's time for dinner," or "it's time for school," or "it's time for bed."

He wondered if Hannah saw him not so much as a parent but as a human alarm clock.

She was ready for school, her backpack at her side, but she was sitting on the bed looking glum.

"Can we talk?" Shay asked, stepping into the room.

She nodded.

"Mrs. Brannigan told me something is troubling you this morning. Is it anything I can help you with?"

She shook her head.

"Can you tell me what's wrong, Hannah?"

"It's nothing," she whispered. "Mrs. Brannigan shouldn't have bothered you."

"You're no bother to me," he said.

She looked askance, as if she didn't believe him.

He sat beside her. "Really," he insisted. "Please, tell me what's wrong. Maybe there's something I can do."

She stood. "There's nothing wrong. I'm ready to go to school now."

"Is this about the kids at school who are bothering you?" he asked, remaining seated.

She shrugged. "Maybe."

"Maybe?" he asked, wanting to understand.

"If Adam went to the same school, he'd make them stop." Her voice dropped. "But it's no big thing. Mrs. B said I need to ignore them."

Something about the way she said "Adam" struck him. Adam was her brother … her half-brother, as it turned out. And then Shay remembered Mrs. Brannigan had specifically mentioned that Hannah was "unable to see her brother." A not-so-subtle hint, perhaps? He patted the spot on the bed where she'd been sitting, and she sat beside him once more.

He waited a long moment before asking, "You miss Adam, don't you?"

He saw tears well up in her eyes, but she looked away, and when she faced him again, they were gone. What a tough little thing she was.

"It's okay," she whispered.

"What if we go find him after school? Let you two say hello? Maybe even take him out for ice cream."

Her small, serious face brightened. "Can we?"

He smiled in return. "I don't see why not."

"Really? You'll be there after school?"

"Yes," he vowed. "In fact, I'll pick you up about a half-hour early so we can meet Adam as he's walking home, rather than going to his house. Do you think that's a good idea?"

Her eyes widened with delight. "Yes, that would be great."

He grinned. He didn't think he had ever heard her so enthusiastic about anything since she'd come to live with him, and that realization caused a sudden lump in his throat. He took a moment to find his voice. "I'll take you to school now and explain to the teachers that you'll be leaving early today."

She nodded, then smiled at him. "Okay."

He wanted so much to do the right thing by her that he found it almost painful.

19

"So," Lorene said that same morning as Rebecca drank her coffee before leaving for work, "your new boyfriend seems to have quite a bit of money. He left a huge tip at the restaurant last night."

"He does," Rebecca said. "And since he's in the business, he knows how important tips are to the staff."

Lorene picked up the morning *Chronicle*. "This is your case, isn't it?" she asked, pointing to the latest story about the missing children. It said that the police seemed baffled by the children's disappearance, and equally at a loss about the father's murder. Not only was there no arrest, they didn't even have any suspects yet.

"Yes." Rebecca tried to drink her coffee fast to get out of there, but it was simply too hot.

"Hmph," was Lorene's only reaction, then she turned to the Food section of the paper.

"Does your new boyfriend's nightclub serve food?" she asked, perusing the recipes even as she said the word 'nightclub' as if it had four letters.

"Expensive appetizers, yes."

Lorene eyed Rebecca, her lips pursed—a common look for her. "I had the impression you had broken up with him, but it seems things are serious between the two of you."

"They are," Rebecca admitted. "I wasn't sure for a while, but now I am."

"I can't say that thrills me," Lorene said. "In fact, I'm disappointed because I came here expecting I'd be giving you great news."

Rebecca put down her coffee cup. "What news?"

"I had hoped you'd be willing to walk away from the life you have here," Lorene said. "In fact, looking around at this little apartment, at this city with a population way to too large for it, and all its accompanying problems, I still feel that way."

"You hope I'd want to leave the city, my job, and friends? Why?"

Lorene drew in her breath a moment. "Ed Lockhart is getting a divorce. He was in Boise last week and stopped by my house. We talked a long time."

Just hearing Lorene speak that name caused years to wash away. Edward Lockhart had been her first boyfriend—the boy next door, the fellow she had been crazy about from the time she was fourteen and first noticed boys. They had started dating when she was seventeen and he was nineteen. She always expected they would marry. But then, everything fell apart.

She didn't want to think about those bitter, hurtful days. "Do you really think I still care about Ed Lockhart?"

"Listen to what I have to say," Lorene interrupted. "Ed admitted to me he had always wanted to join our farm to his. He thought, after you two were married, someday you'd inherit half of it, and eventually you two would buy out Courtney and own it all. Instead, after your father passed away, and I sold it to a stranger. Ed felt betrayed, as if he'd been an idiot for having spent so many years with only one plan in mind. He claims he went off the deep end and became irrationally angry."

"And took his anger out on me." Rebecca remembered how devastated she had felt when Ed broke off their engagement. Whenever she allowed herself to think back on those days soon after her father's death, when she learned that the farm she grew up on, loved, and knew every inch of had been sold, and that the man she'd been in love with most of her life no longer loved her, the sadness and disappointment she had felt was all but crushing.

It was the reason she had left the state to start a new life. She swore she would never again allow anyone so much control over her life or her heart.

Lorene continued. "Ed thought you had a hand in the sale, that you'd encouraged me to sell, despite your denials to him. He was bitter at both of us."

"I don't believe that," Rebecca said. "He knew I was as shocked as anyone that you would sell dad's farm."

Lorene shrugged off Rebecca's denials. "Why would he lie? He also confessed that he had married on the rebound from all that had happened with you and the farm. He realized the woman he married wasn't nearly as nice or attractive as the girl next-door. You, Rebecca—the girl he had grown up with, the girl who had meant everything to him once, and who he now knows still means everything to him."

Rebecca stared hard at Lorene. "I'm sorry for him because that 'girl' no longer exists."

"Are you sure?" Lorene asked. "I know how much you loved him once, and I know, now, he still loves you."

Rebecca grimaced. "He loves me? Yeah, right. He doesn't even know me. Not anymore. This conversation is over."

But Lorene wouldn't stop. "Back then, I was so wrapped up in all the changes in my life, I didn't realize how culpable I was in causing the two of you to breakup. Now that I do, I felt it was my duty to come here and let you know what's going on in his head, and how unhappy all this has made him. If there's any chance you could forgive him for what he did, and to forgive me for what I did, there's a home and there's a man you once loved more than anything waiting for you."

Rebecca stared hard at her mother. "This is my life now, the life I've created for myself, and no matter how it looks to you, I love it." She stood. "And now, I've got to get to work. There are two little kids somewhere in this city that I want to help find."

"Rebecca, you need to think about Ed," Lorene insisted. "You owe him that. And me."

Richie had stewed all night over what to do about Rebecca and her escalating problems with City Hall. That morning, mid-morning actually, he contacted a friend of his mother's named Matteo Veltroni. Veltroni knew everyone who was anyone in city government including the mayor, the deputy mayor, and the entire Board of Supervisors. Every year he was the top contributor to their campaigns and as a result many people saw Veltroni as a master puppeteer with political marionettes at the end of his strings.

Richie thought if anyone might know if or why Dianne Cahill had it in for Rebecca, it would be Veltroni.

The strangest thing about the man, in Richie's point of view, was that he was smitten by Carmela, Richie's mother. Considering that Veltroni could have had any number of young, beautiful women who swirled around him like hummingbirds to a spring flower, Richie couldn't understand why he always made a fuss over Carmela. Maybe the fact she knew how to play hard-to-get added to her allure. Or, at least, Richie hoped she played hard to get.

If she didn't, he didn't want to imagine her and Veltroni together. That was a vision he doubted he could ever "un-see."

But as a result of that "friendship," when Richie gave Veltroni a call and asked if they could meet briefly, Veltroni happily obliged.

The two met at Gino's bar in North Beach, a favorite hangout for many of the city's Italians, even though few of them still lived in the area.

Veltroni was sipping on a rum and coke, heavy on the coke, when Richie arrived. "My stomach," he said by way of explanation.

Richie ordered a gin and tonic, without the gin. "Same reason," he explained.

After a few pleasantries, including Veltroni asking after Carmela, Richie got down to business. "The woman I'm seeing, Rebecca Mayfield, is a homicide detective. She's been involved in some scary incidents lately, and from what I've seen, I suspect someone in City Hall—possibly working with the police commissioner—is behind them."

Veltroni snorted. "What, you mean that *coglione,* Giulio Barcelli, is giving her grief? He'd take out half the city if his bosses told him to."

Richie couldn't help but grin at Veltroni calling the police commissioner a "testicle," a very Italian way of saying the guy's an idiot. "Exactly."

Veltroni's rubbery lips protruded. "I've also heard the Virginia Kirk case is again being talked about."

As usual, Richie thought, Veltroni was on top of things. "It is."

"You should know that Kirk and the Deputy Mayor are friends."

"Virginia Kirk and Dianne Cahill?" Richie exclaimed.

"How else did Kirk get away with murder?"

Richie couldn't stop his eyes from widening.

Veltroni's voice was deep and raspy. "Of course, the woman Kirk killed, that Sharon Lynch, was a real witch, *una strega.* Lots of people said she was weird. A little crazy even, so nobody much cared that she'd been offed except maybe her family."

"That would explain why Kirk is suddenly in the picture again," Richie said.

"You know, Richie, when your lady investigated some recent cases and exposed those big real estate deals, she made everyone run for the hills. And all of them pointed their fingers at everyone else until they found a fall guy—that kid who used to be the mayor's chief of staff, the one they like to pretend killed himself."

Richie nodded. "Right. Sean Hinkle. That much I know. But it doesn't tell me who's behind it all, or why they haven't backed off."

"Is your lady friend working a new case, maybe?" Veltroni asked.

"Her only case is about some guy out in the Bayview, probably offed by his wife. He doesn't seem connected to anyone."

"Maybe, maybe not." Veltroni took out a cheroot, offered one to Richie who turned it down, and then lit it and took a few puffs. Despite the city's no-smoking-indoors policy, no one at Gino's would dare to stop him. "Listen to me, if something's going on that ain't no good, you can bet your bottom dollar they're all in on it. They're *sfachim*—no good. Trust me on that."

Richie knew Veltroni was right.

"But don't tell me nothing about what they're up to," Veltroni continued. "I don't wanna know, at least, not yet. You gotta choose your time, and your enemies, you know. But I warn you, they didn't get rich off city government by being Boy Scouts and Girl Scouts, that's for sure. For Carmela's sake, I don't like to see you get involved. When they're cornered, they can be mean and dangerous."

"Thanks, but backing off on this isn't an option." Richie's words were firm.

Veltroni shut his eyes a moment. "Look, have you ever met Cahill or the mayor?"

"The mayor, yes. But I don't know Cahill."

Veltroni slurped his drink, then looked hard at Richie. He wasn't a heavy man, but his face was dark and loose skinned, especially around his cheeks, lips, and under his black, watery eyes. "Maybe we need to fix that. What if we get the two of them to Big Caesar's? That would be a way for you to see them in action outside of work."

"That would be great," Richie said.

Veltroni took out his cell phone. "You want'em there tonight?"

Richie was surprised. "You can do it that fast?"

"Just watch me." But then Veltroni's rubbery face spread into a wide smile as he added, "As long as you see that Carmela is there, I'll take care of the others."

Richie swallowed hard. "Deal."

20

I nstead of going straight to Homicide and getting caught up in paperwork, red tape, and everything else going on around her desk, Rebecca drove out to Daryl Hawley's house.

Although Jared had spent a lot of time in the neighborhood yesterday, checking out abandoned buildings—even a mortuary, apparently—plus talking to neighbors and shop owners, she wanted to look over the area herself. Also, she needed to get the bitter taste out of her mouth after hearing Lorene's revelations about Ed Lockhart and what had happened years earlier. She was glad she was no longer the young, naive girl that had let those two devastate her. They weren't, she realized now, worth it. And, despite Lorene's words, Rebecca owed them nothing.

The lack of progress in finding the two Hawley children was maddening. The FBI and the SVU had come up with one red herring after the other. There had been no citizen sightings that had panned out, and they were running around like chickens with their heads cut off, even following a lead to Nebraska. The result was a fat goose egg. To Rebecca, their lack of success was unacceptable.

She couldn't help but grow increasingly nervous about what

might have happened to the children. As obnoxious as Tracy Hawley was, Rebecca understood and sympathized with her. She was glad her investigation had, so far at least, cleared Tracy who had a solid alibi for Sunday night, and apparently no funds to pay off a hitman.

She went to small businesses in the area, fast food shops, grocery stores, drug stores, dollar stores, to see if anyone had noticed any customers acting odd lately. It was the sort of thing beat cops usually did, but since she was getting nowhere otherwise, pounding the pavement herself was no waste of time.

Nothing came of it until she entered the corner grocery store about a quarter mile from Daryl Hawley's home.

Except for the owner who, judging from his accent was from India, the store was empty.

She asked her usual questions about his customers.

The owner thought a moment. "Well, I don't want to make any trouble for anyone," he said, his voice mild, "but one of my customers bought some milk earlier in the week."

Rebecca didn't get it. "Milk?"

The grocer pressed his fingertips together. "You see, he never buys that sort of thing. Usually it's beer, canned foods, French bread. And the day before yesterday, he bought even more milk. And Frosted Flakes."

Rebecca's pulse quickened. "Kids."

The grocer nodded. "Kids drink a lot of milk. I know. I have four young ones." The mere mention of them caused his face to brighten. "But as I said, it might mean nothing."

"What's the man's name?"

"I'm sorry I don't know. Some of my customers are chatty. We talk, we share names, tales of our children. But not him. He never says a word beyond hello, goodbye. He comes in, buys a few things, then leaves. Pays cash always. But I'm sure he lives nearby."

"What does he look like?"

"I'd say he's in his forties. Maybe five foot seven or eight, two hundred pounds. That might be too high, but his build is quite ... um ... large. He has long brown hair—shaggy. Brown eyes." The grocer smiled as he added, "My kids would say everything about him is kind of shaggy. Oh, wait. That's not right. Once he wore some kind of uniform."

"A uniform? Like a cop?"

"No, not that type. Not military either. I don't know. Maybe a service provider of some sort? A bus or limo driver? It wasn't dirty enough for a mechanic, but maybe he just had it washed? I'm just not sure."

Everything told Rebecca this was all important information. "Can you get off work to come down to the Hall of Justice so we can get a sketch of this guy?"

"I don't know... my store. Maybe tomorrow morning?"

"I'd like you to come now," she said. "We'll be as fast as we can. If it will help us find the missing children sooner ... every minute counts."

Dark eyes filled with understanding. "I'll lock up."

As they left, Rebecca phoned Lt. Eastwood and asked him to line up the bureau's sketch artist because she had someone who may have seen the kidnapper, and then called Cheryl Wong, the SVU inspector, to let her know about this possible lead.

Much as she tried to sound cautious and skeptical, she could feel it in her blood that this was a good lead. For the first time that day, she felt like the search for the missing kids could be taking a turn for the better.

Shay checked the time. The last thing he wanted to do was to be late picking up Hannah so she could meet her brother. He had even stopped and bought a present for her to give to Adam, some-thing a clerk said a twelve-year-old boy would love: a high-quality skateboard.

He still had a lot of time to kill and took a ride out to see the mortuary where Dianne Cahill and the Blaxor directors met. It puzzled him. Why would they choose a mortuary for their meeting?

He drove to Balou Street and from there widened his search until he found it. It was one hell of an ugly place. He'd hate that to be his last earthly visit before being shut up in a coffin.

He used his phone to log into the city's Office of Assessor-Recorder and discovered that the city owned the building and grounds. They had confiscated it when the owners defaulted on their property taxes. Shay wasn't surprised the business went under. Who would want to be buried by an outfit as miserable as death itself?

He parked his Maserati, walked over to the mortuary, and tried the front doors. They were locked, as expected. He walked along the driveway to another door, a metal one, and found it locked up. Few cobwebs were around the edges of the door, but the city usually did some minimal maintenance on its properties whether or not in use, and often left electricity and running water turned on.

Once Shay reached the back of the lot, he understood why it had been chosen as a meeting place.

The back lot was completely cut off from view by anyone in the street. The buildings that surrounded it were all empty, which meant anyone meeting there could do so free from worry of being seen. Very clever.

Checking his watch, he got back into his car. It was time to pick up Hannah to meet her brother and hopefully, to see her smile again.

21

Rebecca had no sooner introduced the grocer to the sketch artist when she got a call from dispatch. There was another homicide—the last thing she needed, when she finally had a lead on the missing kids—but since she and her partner were the on-call detectives that week, they had no choice but to head to the scene.

She found Jared at his desk doing background checks on Daryl Hawley's associates as well as Tracy Hawley's date. So far, none of them had any red flags associated with their names.

"A body's been found in the St. Francis Wood area," Rebecca said. "Ready?"

Jared looked surprised, but immediately stood and put on his jacket. "Absolutely."

Rebecca drove to the crime scene and couldn't help but reflect how different this one was from the scene that began her week. The house was a two-story, cream-colored stucco with French windows, shutters, and elaborate black iron grillwork as a security gate.

Even the police presence securing the crime scene seemed more sedate than in the Bayview-Hunters Point area. No neighbors stood around trying to see what was going on, although Rebecca spotted several standing at their windows.

A uniformed officer met the detectives and handed them booties as they entered the house. The foyer was larger than Rebecca's entire apartment.

To the left was an elaborately and expensively furnished living room.

On the floor, marring the beauty of the room, lay a woman. She was face up with a large knife protruding from her midsection, right below the rib cage. From the amount of blood on her and the surrounding floor, and the angle of the knife, it most likely penetrated her heart. She had been attractive, mid-forties, brunette, and dressed in a jogging outfit.

"Who is she?" Rebecca asked.

"Paula Forsyth," the officer told her. "The cleaning lady discovered her, and she's now in the kitchen in a bit of a shock. Forsyth is married, but her husband travels a lot. The cleaning lady has no idea if he's even in the country."

Just then, Dr. Evelyn Ramirez, the medical examiner showed up with her technicians. Rebecca greeted her, introduced her to Jared, and then left the room for Ramirez to study the body.

Rebecca and Jared went to the cleaning lady. She spoke little English and seemed afraid of having anything to do with the police. Rebecca understood the situation and spoke slowly and gently. She learned the woman worked at the home only on Mondays and Thursdays, and the house was always empty when she did her job, Rebecca doubted the poor woman knew much about what went on in this household, and all their questions confirmed it.

Rebecca moved on to the den and Jared the master bedroom as they searched for computers, paperwork, cell phones, anything that told them who the woman was, let alone why anyone would want to kill her.

Rebecca stared with surprise as she went through Forsyth's handbag and found business cards showing she was the vice president of Blaxor Pharmaceuticals.

Blaxor ... that was where Tracy Hawley worked. And where Tracy's Sunday evening date worked. Could there possibly be a connection between Daryl Hawley's murder and this one? Looking around the room where she stood, Rebecca couldn't imagine it, but she also couldn't believe the deaths were a simple coincidence.

A quick glance out the window told her the press were already arriving.

She already was doing all she could to avoid reporters. They knew she almost never answered any of their questions, and simply referred them to the department's press office. But the longer the children remained missing and their father's killer at large, the harder it was to avoid their questions.

And now, her having the lead in Paula Forsyth's death would make a bad situation ten times worse. Given Forsyth's position, the so-called "high society" in the city most likely knew her, which would make the media more demanding than ever that Rebecca be the one to directly answer their questions, not some PR person who didn't know any of the details. More than ever, Rebecca wished Bill Sutter was still on the job so he could talk to the reporters—a duty he genuinely enjoyed.

She and Jared had a lot of work to do and needed to do it quickly. Society didn't like it when they realized a killer had targeted one of their own.

∼

Hannah knew the route Adam took to walk home from school. When Shay spotted him with a group of friends, he parked the car a little ahead of the boys, and Hannah got out holding the present in her hands.

She and Adam hugged each other, both wearing broad smiles. As Shay looked at Hannah's face, he realized how much she loved and missed her brother. He hadn't thought of how both children had not only lost their mother but also each other. He vowed to find a way to for them to spend time together.

Adam opened the present and was overjoyed. He tried out the fancy skateboard, riding up and down the sidewalk, and declared it great, much to Hannah's delight. But then, as his friends took turns on it, Adam pulled Hannah aside.

As he spoke, her demeanor changed. She seemed to stand stiffer, straighter, and several times vehemently shook her head. Finally, looking stricken, she turned from him, ran back to Shay's car, and got in.

Shay watched her, but also Adam, who swaggered back to his friends and was now, with his skateboard, the center of attention.

"Do you want to leave?" Shay asked Hannah.

She nodded, staring straight ahead.

Shay started engine, but he no sooner pulled out of the parking space than he couldn't take her silence. Keeping his eyes on the busy streets as he drove, he said, "You looked happy to see Adam ... at first."

"Yes," she whispered.

"And he seemed happy, too."

"Yes."

"But it looked like something happened between you."

She shrugged.

"Would you like to see him more often?" Shay asked.

She made no response.

"Yes?" He prompted.

She took a moment, then said, "Adam told me we can't. He's not even going to tell Papa, I mean, Gebran, that I gave him a present. He said I can no longer be his sister, and that I must forget about him."

Shay felt his anger rise. He hated the pain he heard in her words. "Why would he say such a thing?"

"Papa told him I have 'bad blood,' and so does Mama."

Shay was furious, and disgusted. What kind of man would say such a thing? He would love to wrap his hands around Gebran's fat neck for saying such words about this sensitive child. He tried hard to tamp down his outrage, but before he could find anything comforting to say, Hannah continued. "I told him it's not true. But he said I was wrong to question Papa. He said Mama and I are dead to them both."

Shay looked over at her. He saw no tears, only toughness and bravery. "I'm so sorry," he murmured.

"I don't think Papa means it," Hannah whispered, then turned her head away from him, facing the passenger window as he drove them home.

22

Rebecca was in the Forsyth home gathering evidence and trying to reach Paula Forsyth's husband in Shanghai, China, when her mother phoned.

"Rebecca, something terrible has happened." Lorene sounded breathless.

"Are you all right?"

"Two men broke into your apartment," Lorene cried. "They rang the bell, and I went down the breezeway and opened the door to let them in. But they pushed me and acted like they were about to attack. Somehow, I broke free and ran out to the street. I got away!"

"My God! Did they chase you? Where are you?"

"I ran to the corner and hid inside the laundromat. In a few minutes, I saw them leave and drive away. I think they might have gone inside your apartment, but I'm not sure if they robbed it. I went inside just long enough to grab my purse and cell phone so I could call you. I'm now in a coffee shop on Jones and Bush streets. There are a lot of cars and people, so I'm safe here, right?"

"What about Spike?" Rebecca asked. "Is he okay?"

"I … I don't know. I didn't see him. Maybe he's hiding."

"Did you shut the door behind you?"

"I don't remember!"

"Go back, shut it so he won't run out into the street if he's scared."

"I can't go back there! What if they come again?"

"All right, stay put. But tell me, what did these men look like?"

"I don't know—big guys, filthy baseball caps on their heads, dark glasses, tattoos, lots of silver stuff in their nostrils and ears. Really disgusting. They drove a black SUV. Whatever possessed me to come here! Things like this don't happen in Boise."

Rebecca drew in her breath. "Okay. Stay put. I'll come get you as soon as I can."

Someone breaking into her apartment had shades of the problems she'd been having over the past few months, not to mention the shooting just days before. Someone was tightening the screws.

She phoned Richie, hoping he might be near her apartment.

She immediately told him about the break-in and her mother's reaction. "She's all right," Rebecca said, "but I'm worried about Spike. I'm at a crime scene on the other side of town. I'll leave as soon as I can but, by chance, are you close to my place?"

"In fact, I am."

Rebecca suddenly heard: —*Richie, how can you ask me such a thing?*–

"You're with your mother, I take it," Rebecca said, recognizing Carmela's voice bellowing in the background.

"I'm at her house, and happy to leave it," he said.

—*Leave? You think it's fine to disrupt my entire day and then walk away?* –

"If you're in the middle of something," Rebecca began, wondering why Carmela sounded so upset.

"No!" He all but shouted into the phone. "I'm going right now."

He hung up.

Rebecca didn't understand what was going on, but she was more than glad he would check on Spike. She loved the little guy.

As soon as she could, she gave Jared a long list of instructions on what to do, and then left the crime scene. She was driving home when Richie phoned. She put him on speaker.

"I found Spike under your bed. He's fine."

"Thank you. What a relief."

"Are you coming home?"

"Yes, but I've got to make one quick stop at Homicide."

"Your mother's not here," he added.

"Be thankful."

Back at Homicide, Rebecca rushed to the sketch artist's desk to learn the drawing was finished and the grocer had returned to his store.

She picked up the sketch. It was no one she recognized. "I'll get this out to all patrol units in the area," she said, thanking the artist for his efforts.

She printed out some copies of the sketch, put a few on Jared's desk, stuffed others into her shoulder bag for her interviews, then called Cheryl Wong to tell her the original sketch was being walked to her desk so the SVU could make distribution to their people and street officers. She again mentioned that the man might be wearing some kind of uniform, probably a service or some type of shop uniform, but what type exactly, she didn't know.

After that, she hurried to the coffee shop where Lorene waited. She thought it best not to tell her mother that the "safe place" she had picked to wait was in the heart of the Tenderloin. The less Lorene knew about the rough area, the better.

When they returned to her apartment, Rebecca found Richie

with Spike curled up on his lap, the TV on and tuned to a sports station. The little dog looked blissfully content.

Relieved, Rebecca ran to her dog, hugged and kissed him and Richie both. "Thank you for taking care of him," she said to Richie.

"No problem. I'd been wishing for an excuse to leave my mom's place, and like magic, you phoned."

Rebecca quickly perused her apartment. Nothing seemed to be missing. "It looks as if whoever broke in wasn't here to rob me," she said with a worried frown.

"Who would waste their time breaking into a place like this?" Lorene scoffed.

Richie put his hand on Rebecca's back and led her away from Lorene's vitriol before a war broke out. "It looks to me," he said, "as if someone was looking for you, or they planned to wait until you turned up."

"It makes little sense," Rebecca said.

"Except that someone's been after you for a while now," he added as he shut off the television.

"What?" Lorene screeched. "Someone's after you and you left me alone in your apartment?"

"I didn't think it was dangerous," Rebecca told her. "I'm often here alone."

"But you've got a gun. If this was Idaho, I'd have one, too," Lorene wailed. "People warned me I'd be in big trouble if I got caught with a concealed weapon in this state, even though I have an Idaho permit. Why did I listen to them?"

"You can shoot?" Richie looked at her in surprise.

"Of course," she said, giving him a steely eyed stare, hands on hips. "If someone came by causing trouble way out where I lived, calling nine-one-one wasn't exactly a good option."

The look Richie gave her said he wouldn't mess with her even if she didn't have a gun.

At the same time, Rebecca was on the phone telling Lt. Eastwood about the break-in. He knew of the previous attacks on her, but he was aghast to learn her mother had been in the apartment alone.

"I'll send some CSI technicians over to see if they can find fingerprints or any other clues as to who might be behind this," Eastwood said. "In the meantime, do you have someplace else to go? It might not be safe for your mother to be there while you're working."

Rebecca glanced at Richie. She couldn't think of anywhere safer. "We do. We'll be fine."

When the call ended, she faced Richie and Lorene. "Some techs will come by to look for fingerprints and the other evidence. And we need to find a place to stay for a while."

"Exactly," Richie said. "Glad Eastwood finally has some sense. Time to pack a few things."

"Where are we going?" Lorene's gaze narrowed as she looked from one to the other.

"To Richie's house," Rebecca said. She figured that was enough explanation for now.

"Wait a minute!" Lorene followed Rebecca into the bedroom. "It's clear you're in some kind of danger. I don't think running off to your boyfriend's house is enough. It's time for you to forget all this nonsense and come home."

Rebecca began packing her belongings. "This is my home."

"No, it isn't! It's madness for you to continue to put your life in danger. What if I wasn't here? What would have happened if you were the one who opened the door? Or if they broke in and when you came home they were here waiting for you?"

"Mom, stop. I know you're worried, but—"

"But nothing! Okay, I made mistakes in the past. I should have at least explained myself to you. Not that I had to. I mean, you were still young, and it was *my* farm. But if you get yourself killed in this city because I drove you away from the farm and Ed, I'd never forgive myself."

"Ed? Who's Ed?" Richie asked.

Rebecca looked up and saw he was standing in the doorway watching … and listening.

"You two were made for each other," Lorene said, ignoring Richie. "You were the cutest couple ever—everyone said so. He's come to his senses and it's time you did, too. Come home with me, Rebecca!"

"What's all this?" Richie studied Rebecca.

She faced him, furious at her mother's words. "It's ancient history, that's what. A part of my life that's over and has been for years." She turned to Lorene. "I'm staying. You can go back to Idaho now if you want. Or, you can come with me to Richie's. It's your choice."

Lorene folded her arms. "I'm not leaving when you're in danger. I'll pack my things, which will take about two seconds because I haven't really unpacked yet. But … is his place big enough? I don't know if I like the idea of staying in some 'bachelor pad.'" The last two words dripped from her tongue.

"It's big enough, believe me," Rebecca muttered, then zipped up her suitcase.

Richie frowned as he watched the exchange. She hated that he had heard all that.

"Paula Forsyth is dead," Dianne Cahill said into the phone. "Murdered."

"I just heard," Clive Hutchinson said. "I can't believe it."

"Can't you?" Dianne spat out the words. "You've always been worried about her."

"Only because of Mayfield," Hutchinson said. "I thought you

were upping the pressure on her? How's that working out?" His voice was all but a sneer.

"I don't see you stepping up to help," she yelled.

"Help? I've done more than enough." It sounded as if Hutchinson spoke through gritted teeth, trying his best to keep his voice low. Then he loudly sucked in his breath. "I'm sick of all of you."

"Ready to cut and run now that you've gotten a big promotion. It's the sort of thing a coward would do, and you've always been a coward, Clive."

"Coward?"

"You're afraid to see me."

"Listen, just because I've been busy lately—"

"Don't give me that," she shrieked, then stopped, her voice turning low and harsh. "Do you really think I'm so stupid? Do you think I don't have spies all over this city who are more than happy to give me every sordid detail about you?" It was all she could do not to give in to tears. Tears of anger. Tears of sorrow and disappointment.

"Maybe we can meet." Clive sounded oh, so reasonable. "Let's talk about this. And what we should do about it."

"Meet you?" Her voice went soft a moment, then she steeled her spine. "I don't think I dare to."

"Screw you, Dianne! I can say the same about you. And with a hell of a lot better reason!"

"On the other hand," she said, her tone suddenly tougher, brighter, "Matteo Veltroni invited the mayor and me to Big Caesar's tonight. Why don't you join us?"

He sucked in his breath. "I suppose this is an order."

"If that's how you want to hear it."

23

Caravan-like in their respective cars, Richie in the lead, followed by Rebecca, and then Lorene, they crossed the city. Richie pulled into his driveway and waited for the other two to park. He had long wanted Rebecca to move in with him, but this wasn't the way he had envisioned it happening.

Still, he'd take it.

After spending about ten minutes with Lorene, he understood why she and Rebecca weren't close. But he also understood Lorene's worry and unhappiness over Rebecca's situation. He felt the same way.

He also thanked God that whoever had broken in while Lorene was in the apartment hadn't feared her as a potential witness and shot her on the spot. He couldn't imagine the guilt Rebecca would have felt if such a thing had happened.

His take on the two was that Lorene could be bossy, judgmental, and irritating, and Rebecca could be stubborn and willful, but deep down both had the other's interests at heart. He mainly hoped Lorene would decide that coming to the city had been a big mistake, and after seeing that Rebecca was living safely in his house, would go back to Idaho. Like, maybe, in the next hour or two.

"The city looks much prettier and cleaner from up here," Lorene said, admiring the view as Richie took her suitcase from her car. She followed him up the stairs. "What do you call this area? Twin Peaks?"

"That's it," he said.

"Where Rebecca lives is so grungy and loud and filled with tourists, I don't see how she stands it. A nice place to visit, perhaps, but living there ..." She continued talking as she entered the house, but then stopped cold.

"This is lovely." Lorene's brows crossed in surprise as she stepped into his spacious living room and eyed a large, expensive-looking sofa and loveseat, coordinated accent chairs in soft blues and grays, a fireplace, and a picture window with an even better view than from street level. "You live here alone?"

"I do."

"You must be divorced. Was this where you lived with your wife?"

Richie gave Rebecca a confused glance. "I've never been married," he said, then frowned. "Does my house look that feminine?"

"No. But it's much too nice for a bachelor."

Richie was momentarily speechless. For all Lorene's chatter, the only thing he really wanted to hear from her was about this strange "Ed." But maybe that would be best handled when Rebecca wasn't around.

"Let me show you your bedroom. It's actually a suite," Richie said as he led her past the kitchen to a guest room on the opposite side of the house from the other bedrooms. When he had the home remodeled, he purposefully set up a bedroom, bathroom, and even a little sitting area over the garage in case his mother ever came to live with him in her old age. He'd seen it happen often with his buddies, and he wanted to be sure, if he were in that situation, that he could retain as much privacy as possible.

And right now, keeping Lorene away from him and Rebecca seemed like a good idea.

∼

As Lorene went off to unpack and to lie down after her harrowing experience at Rebecca's apartment, Rebecca and Richie went out to his deck.

It was a small area with three chairs overlooking a simple lawn and garden. Flowers and shrubs grew along the fences and a sunny corner held a small vegetable garden with tomatoes, peppers, zucchini, and lots of herbs, garlic, and onions. Sometimes she forgot what a good cook Richie was when he took the time to make them a meal from scratch. Carmela had taught him well.

Richie had grabbed some beer from the fridge, and as they sat, he popped open the bottles, and handed her one.

She took a sip as she looked out at his garden. Maybe because Lorene had brought up the past, Rebecca's thoughts turned to her early days with Richie and the first time she'd come out here with him. He had been accused of murder and, inexplicably, had turned to her for help. They were handcuffed together and, despite the ridiculousness of the situation, she remembered how defeated he had seemed, how down in spirit, and yet so innocent of the charges.

She studied him now. Although his black hair might have a few strands of gray, he wore it long enough to show its soft waves. And while his thin face had a few lines around his mouth and eyes, he was, to her, rakishly handsome.

They had come a long way together.

"Any news on the missing kids?" he asked, understanding what most bothered her at the moment.

"No. And things are getting more complicated because of this latest murder." She then told him about Paula Forsyth, and how she was vice president at Blaxor Pharmaceuticals—the same place where Daryl Hawley's wife worked.

"Paula Forsyth is dead?" Richie asked.

"Yes. I guess it hasn't hit the news yet." She eyed him. "You knew her?"

He bit his bottom lip a moment. "Not exactly." She listened with growing amazement as he told her about Vito following Dianne Cahill to the empty lot behind the Ventura Brothers Mortuary where she met with Blaxor's Paula Forsyth and Varg Hague. "But I had no idea," he said, "that there was a connection between your victim, Daryl Hawley and Blaxor."

"Only that his wife worked there," Rebecca said.

"Hmm," was Richie's only response as he stared out over the garden.

She could almost see the wheels churning in his head, and she couldn't help but wonder if he had already learned far more about these people than she'd been able to dig up—and if there wasn't something very fishy about Blaxor. "But why in the world," she asked, "would the city's deputy mayor hold a secret meeting with them?"

"I suspect it has to do with a drug called Lulz—an anti-depressant," Richie said. "I think the city gives it out in homeless shelters, mainly to help people cope with anxiety. From what Shay found out, it's a fairly weak drug, and expensive. No generics yet to keep down the price."

"That's crazy."

"I'll tell you what else is crazy. Dianne Cahill is friends with Virginia Kirk. And since Kirk suddenly decided to file a lawsuit against the city because of you and Bill Sutter, I can see the hand of our beloved deputy mayor in that as well."

Rebecca's blood boiled. "I never warmed up to Dianne Cahill, for good reason, it appears. Something tells me the deputy mayor is keeping dark secrets and has a lot to answer for."

Once sure her mother was settled in Richie's capable hands, Rebecca returned to Homicide to work on Paula Forsyth's murder. She had already taken two calls from Jared and ignored three from Lt. Eastwood. She didn't want to ignore a fourth. Also, she planned to look into Blaxor Pharmaceuticals as well as into Daryl Hawley's job of delivering pharmaceutical products. The possibility of a bigger connection seemed remote, but equally hard to imagine the two deaths were a mere coincidence.

Once at work, Eastwood told her to put aside the Hawley case and concentrate on Paula Forsyth's murder. She knew his "reasoning" was all about the publicity one case would get over the other. She did her best to explain to Eastwood the connection between the Hawley and Forsyth murders.

"You can pursue that for a day," Eastwood said, sucking in his cheeks. "But if nothing develops, you concentrate on the Forsyth murder. Is that understood?"

"Yes, sir," she muttered, then returned to her desk.

She reached the owner of RX Wholesale by phone. "Mr. Owens, Inspector Mayfield here. I'm sorry to bother you in the evening, but I need a complete list of the medical supplies Daryl Hawley delivered and the places he delivered them in the two weeks before his death. I'm hoping you can pull the data and email it to me as soon as possible."

"Are you kidding?" Owens bellowed. "It's on the computer and my secretary's already gone home for the day."

"I'm sure someone else in your office will be able to find it easily and quickly."

"You aren't suggesting my supplies or my customers are in any way involved in Hawley's death, are you?"

"I'll know more as soon as I get the data I requested. If you still have my card, it's got my email."

She was glad he didn't complain so much she had to remind him of exactly how serious a crime this was.

Not twenty minutes later, she received the email with the requested information. A quick perusal of the list showed her that Hawley routinely delivered the Blaxor drug, Lulz, to several medicine dispensaries and clinics run by the city.

She searched for more information about the drug, and its high price stunned her.

"You look lost in thought, Mayfield." Jared sat down in the guest chair by her desk.

She hadn't expected to find him returning to work after dinner. She guessed she simply wasn't used to a partner being as eager to work a case as she was.

"I'm looking into a drug called Lulz. Have you ever heard of it?"

"Lulz? Whatever are you doing looking into drugs?" His expression turned into a frown. "And why now?"

She didn't appreciate his tone. "It's a Blaxor product. One Daryl Hawley distributed."

"Oh?" He frowned a moment. "So this Lulz might be a connection between Daryl Hawley and Paula Forsyth? Is that what you think?"

"It's worth checking on."

"How did you find out about it?" Jared's face filled with suspicion.

She didn't know why, but something made her stop trying to explain herself, and especially not to mention Richie's connection to all this. "Research. Some weird stuff I stumbled across. What we know is Daryl Hawley worked for a medical supply distributor that handled it, his wife worked for the company that manufactured it, and now that company's vice president has been murdered." She purposefully left out Richie's discovery of Dianne Cahill's meeting with Forsyth and Hague. Did that mean she didn't trust her new partner? As much as she wanted to, she couldn't—and she wasn't sure why. She hoped she didn't sound too defensive as she added, "Given all that, it seems like a good place to start."

His eyes narrowed. "I expect Hawley's employer distributed all kinds of drugs to all kinds of people. That the city was one of their customers doesn't mean a thing."

That statement floored her and she couldn't help but ask, "How did you know the city was an RX Wholesale customer?"

He drew in his breath. "Didn't you just say that?"

"No. Have you been looking into RX Wholesale?"

He looked sheepish. "You caught me."

Her lips tightened. "And what did you find out?"

"Nothing," he said with a casual shrug. "Not yet, anyway."

She made no comment, but she was growing tired of that answer from him. As she tried to think of one thing he'd learned that contributed to this investigation, despite all the time he spent in the field, on his computer, and on the phone, she couldn't come up with a single piece of evidence or even a clue.

24

F reddie carried a bag with four bologna sandwiches and a carton of milk down the stairs to the basement. Under his arm was the checkers game. He hoped this friendly gesture would end the cries and obnoxious behavior of the prior day. He thought these kids would like him by now. Maybe there was something wrong with them.

He sat on the floor and asked Porter and Molly to join him. They did.

The two then stared at him in silence as he took out one waxed paper wrapped sandwich for each and filled their Dixie cups with milk.

"Here's your dinner," he said jovially. "Now, don't eat everything at once. I made extra sandwiches for you for tomorrow morning. But you need to drink the milk today. It'll spoil overnight since it's not refrigerated."

The children each took a sandwich.

Porter was the first to unwrap his. "It's baloney."

"I don't like baloney," Molly said. "I hope I have something better."

"It's all baloney," Freddie shouted. "All kids like baloney, and if you don't, girl, that's too damn bad. It's all you're getting."

Molly began to cry.

"Will you *stop* that goddamn crying!" he shrieked.

To his amazement, she not only stopped, but took a bite from the sandwich.

She might not be crying any longer, but she was trembling. She was scared of him, but he couldn't imagine why.

She was no fun, he thought. And she was most likely too young to understand checkers, anyway. It was a difficult game.

Maybe he needed a better little girl. Maybe an older one—one who was around Porter's age. Maybe …

He smiled as he thought back on his activities earlier that afternoon.

After only one glance, he had felt immediate hatred for the big, blond fellow who had come poking his nose around the mortuary and back lot. Just what was he doing out there? With his fancy neck scarf and ritzy sports jacket, the guy looked like one of those smug hotshots who had everything—classy clothes, a fabulous car, a trim body. Hell, he even had great hair.

But why had Blondie been interested in this building? Freddie needed to find out. He ran to his car and trailed Blondie all the way across the city. A Maserati wasn't easy to lose sight of, and in city traffic he could keep up with it.

He snorted with derision. Blondie had been so stuck on himself he hadn't even noticed he was being followed. A guy like that paid no attention to an old, beat up Chevy. Few people did.

To his surprise, Blondie drove to a school. And not just any school, but a fancy lah-di-dah private school. Freddie watched him go inside. Minutes later he came back out with a girl who was obviously his daughter.

She wasn't exactly pretty although she was interesting looking with a hint of olive to her otherwise pale skin—just enough to give her a slightly exotic look. But she also had the most capti-vating eyes he had ever seen.

He'd love a daughter with eyes like that.

He bet the fancy man didn't pay much attention to her. Hell, he didn't even let her finish taking her classes. The school day wasn't over and Blondie had pulled her out. Most likely for his own convenience.

He bet Blondie didn't care nearly enough about that girl—doubted he loved her as much as his Maserati, for example.

Nobody would love the little girl with beautiful eyes the way he would.

He bet she could play checkers, too. He chuckled. Maybe she'd even have a chance at beating him. Or at least making a game of it.

Then, they could all be like a family. A real family. Not like those dolls that just sat there and looked so beautiful. No, his family would talk to him, and play with him. But he really didn't like the way Molly kept crying. Maybe she should be replaced. And he now knew who to replace her with.

He smiled as he thought of how Blondie would react when the girl vanished. It'd serve him right.

He faced the two children he already had. "Now, while you eat," he tried to sound gentle, "I'm going to explain the rules of checkers, and then we'll play a game or two."

Molly and Porter eyed each other a moment, then drank their milk and ate their sandwiches without further comment as Freddie carefully explained how to set up a checkerboard.

25

R ichie and Carmela were the first to arrive for the evening's gathering at Big Caesar's. Richie led his mother to the table reserved for the city dignitaries. "Would you like a drink, Ma?" Richie asked. "Some calamari appetizers, maybe?"

"What, you think I'm going to sit all alone at that big table like some *buffone?* No way! I'll wait in your office so you can bring me some coffee and something sweet. And I can take off these damn shoes. I don't know why I bought them, except that they are cute. And they go perfectly with this dress. But, *madonna,* they hurt!"

"But 'Matty' might want to dance," Richie said. Matteo Veltroni only allowed his closest friends to call him Matty. Richie knew Carmela was among them. He, however, was not.

"I'm not stopping him," she said, giving Richie a look he would have considered the "evil eye" if it had come from anyone other than his own mother.

He got her settled in his office, which was large and featured all the comforts of home, and then left for the ballroom to make sure everything was perfect for his important guests.

Soon, Dianne Cahill arrived on the arm of an older, thin, and balding fellow. Richie had heard that she had never married but did have someone special in her life. If that unimposing guy was her "significant other" he understood why she kept him a secret.

"Madame Deputy, welcome to Big Caesars," he said as he introduced himself.

After a few nice words about the club, Cahill said, "This is my assistant, Myron Swain. He's also my brother-in-law. My sister, Myrtle, will be joining us. She had to make a pit stop."

Richie showed them to their table and immediately asked that another place be set.

He had no sooner finished taking care of them than Mayor Cornelius Warren and his wife arrived. The wife—Richie couldn't remember her name—was a skinny, nervous woman who looked as if she'd learned hair, make-up, and couture in the early 1980s and hadn't progressed a decade since.

Richie had met Warren a few times and, ever the politician, Warren greeted him as if they were BFFs.

"I've always wanted to come to Big Caesar's," Mrs. Warren gushed when Richie greeted her. "But I could never get Cornelius to take me. I'm thrilled to be here!"

"Thank you," Richie said, showing them to their seats.

Some minutes later, to Richie's amazement, Clive Hutchinson, the mayor's new chief of staff, arrived. He was tall and distinguished looking with brown hair graying at the temples, black-framed glasses, and wearing an expensive light gray Italian suit. With him was an auburn-haired, twenty-something, curvaceous woman who was, in Richie's estimation, a knockout.

As more place settings were quickly added, Richie couldn't help but notice that Dianne Cahill had grown silent and her pale mocha-colored skin grew positively ashen as she looked at the beautiful woman on Hutchinson's arm.

Hutchinson scarcely glanced at her after quickly greeting everyone at the table and introducing his date, Samantha Turpin.

Despite that, Cahill continued to stare at him. The look she gave him was a mixture of both sorrow and adulation.

Although small talk was being made, as the others around the table became aware of Cahill's fixation on Hutchinson, the atmosphere grew increasingly tense. When Dianne Cahill reached for her wineglass, she wasn't looking and knocked it with the back of her fingers. It teetered but before it fell, Richie grabbed it and righted it.

Cahill's expression was vacant as she murmured something about being clumsy.

"Not at all," he said, and then stood. With all the charm he could muster, he held out his hand. "Seems to me a dance is in order."

Her eyes, overly bright and emotional, met his. The band was playing "Fly Me to the Moon," and Cahill looked at him as if she were coming back from some far off, horrible place. She nodded, giving him a small smile of gratitude as she placed her hand in his and allowed him to lead her to the dance floor.

She danced beautifully, and he found her much more fragile and attractive than he had ever imagined. He chatted about his club and the acts that he had booked, being careful not to question her or cause her to need to make any kind of comment as she slowly regained her composure. Finally, with her head held high, she allowed him to walk her back to the table.

They reached it just in time for Matteo Veltroni's grand entrance. Two men had come in with him, but they stopped by the entrance to the ballroom as if standing guard. It was all Richie could do not to closely inspect the way their jackets fit to see if they were packing. Actually, he expected they were. Veltroni was that kind of guy ... unfortunately.

Veltroni greeted everyone, then took a seat, his gaze and slight frown riveted not he empty seat next to him. "So, Richie, you aren't going to disappoint me, are you?" His tone was light but Richie could see the danger behind Veltroni's black eyes.

"Of course not! I'll go get her."

Richie hurried to his office. "Okay, Ma, he's here. Time for your grand entrance."

"God, Richie, the things I do for you!" She bent over and tried to get her foot into the glittery gold shoe. Richie winced as he watched her. "I think my feet got a little swollen sitting here. I can't get the shoes on."

Hands pressed to the sides of his head, he paced from one end of the office to the other. "You've got to! I mean ... he's waiting."

"You expect me to go out there barefoot?" she yelled.

"It'd be better than not going out there at all!" he shouted right back.

"*Mamaluk'!* You talk to your mother like that, and then you expect me to help you?"

"Please, Ma." He flung his arms wide. "The guy likes you, what can I do?"

She finally jammed her feet in the shoes and then stood. "I've got an idea," she said. "Do you need him to stay with you and those other people out there?"

He paled. He couldn't let her go off alone with that lecherous Lothario ... could he? "It'd be good if he stays."

"*Bene,*" she said with a sigh. "*Andiamo!*"

Veltroni stood, beaming, as she approached. Richie didn't know how she could even walk in those tight shoes, but he chalked it up to another of the many things he would never understand about women.

"Carmela, *cara mia!*" Veltroni's voice boomed.

"Matty, *mio tesoro!*" Carmela sounded equally pleased to see him.

He kissed her on both cheeks, and she returned his greeting, while Richie gaped at his mother calling that old racketeer "her treasure."

Veltroni proudly introduced Carmela to the rest of the group.

As they sat down and ordered drinks, Richie made sure the appetizers and the drinks flowed non-stop. He took a seat on the opposite end of the table from Veltroni so he could get to know the politicians, who they seemed closest to, and how they interacted.

Richie immediately proposed a toast to the group to make them feel welcome, and he was given an okay by the mayor to announce to the other customers (who had already been buzzing about the mayor's presence), that indeed the club was "honored" by the presence of the city's mayor and "our beautiful deputy mayor."

With that, Dianne Cahill's deep brown eyes warmed as she smiled at him, although the look vanished almost as quickly when she glanced at Hutchinson and saw he wasn't paying the slightest bit of attention.

Richie was finding this cabal surprisingly interesting. From their chitchat he quickly picked up that Myron Swain seemed to know everyone who was anyone within city government as well as all the dirt on each of them. But since he had the personal charisma and charm of a dirty dishrag, he could never be a politician. Instead, he needed someone to front for him. Dianne Cahill was clearly that person with her looks and personality and position.

Richie was good at picking out of a group like this who was the leader and who was hanging on by a toenail. He guessed that as soon as Mayor Cornelius Warren got out of the way, Dianne Cahill would run the city with Myron Swain steering her every step of the way. If Cahill was the person behind the attacks on Rebecca, that could be a major problem. He wondered how a homicide inspector, high as the position was, could withstand being her target.

Soon, Veltroni and Carmela got up to dance to "My Funny Valentine." As Richie turned to watch them, he guessed his mother's shoes weren't as painful as she had claimed they were.

"I don't see why we're here," Myron Swain murmured softly to Dianne after Hutchinson and his date went, hand-in-hand, to the dance floor.

The words caught Richie's attention, and he listened to their conversation.

"You know why." Dianne's voice was curt. "We need to keep Veltroni happy."

"The old fart makes me sick," Myron said. "The way he lords it—"

"Stop. Both of you," Myrtle Swain said. She sat on Myron's far side. Compared to her sister, Dianne, Myrtle seemed plain, even mousy. "This is supposed to be a nice evening out."

"And it might be if your sister would stop staring at Hutchinson like a lovesick schoolgirl," Myron barked.

"Leave her alone," Myrtle said.

"She's making a fool of herself," Myron insisted.

"And that bothers you, does it?" Dianne sounded furious, but also hurt.

With that, the trio went quiet.

Richie felt strangely sorry for Cahill. She obviously cared a lot—probably loved—Hutchinson, only to find he was dating someone else. And she seemed to loathe Myron Swain, yet if she had any desire to run for mayor, she would need Myron's connections and expertise.

Although Richie had not previously met Myron Swain, he had heard his reputation as a slimeball. One look at him, and he could tell it was true.

The things we do for love and power, Richie thought, with a mental shake of the head.

Speaking of love … all of a sudden he realized he'd been so wrapped up in the conversations around him, he had failed to notice that Veltroni and his mother were no longer on the dance floor.

He jumped to his feet and scoured the rest of the massive room, but didn't see them anywhere.

Veltroni's two "assistants" remained at the entrance to the club, so Richie knew the man had to still be somewhere inside.

A cold chill ran down his back. Were they in his office? If so, for what purpose? He excused himself from the table and dashed to the side hallway. When he reached the office door, he froze. He hated to go in, to possibly interrupt something he preferred not to think about. But even worse, he hated the thought of *not* interrupting whatever was going on.

Finally, he rattled the doorknob as long as he could without being too obvious about what he was doing, then swung open the door.

Carmela sat at one end of the sofa, her shoes off and her feet up on an ottoman. Veltroni sat at the opposite end with his shoes off as well. On a tray between them was a big bowl of popcorn and a bottle of Chablis. On the TV were reruns of *The Dean Martin Show.*

Both were watching the show and chuckling. "'Ey, Richie," Veltroni said. "Why don't you join us? Dino, he always sang like a bird. Nobody better but Frank, God rest his soul. This is much better than sitting with those *buttagoots'*. And your mother makes popcorn with enough real butter that it melts in your mouth. *Ma, che bella!*"

Richie's eyebrows rose as he glanced at Carmela. She popped a piece of popcorn into her mouth and gave him the biggest shit-eating grin he'd ever seen.

26

Richie got home a little before three a.m. His nightclub closed at two, and he stuck around to lock up. Most nights he left all that to his manager, Tommy Ginnetti. Tonight, he let Tommy leave early. Not so much because he was feeling like Mr. Nice Guy, but he was in no hurry to get home. He didn't care to see Lorene, and he had no idea what time Rebecca would return from work, or if she'd be pulling an all-nighter. He knew the two lost kids were bothering her a lot more than she admitted.

Besides that, his head was spinning with all he'd taken in about the mayor and deputy. What pieces of work they were. And their spouses and others around them weren't much better. The only decent one in the bunch seemed to be Clive Hutchinson who, after a few slow, seductive dances to old favorites like "It Had to be You," and "Tenderly," and left the club with his gorgeous date. Richie understood why.

But after he left, Dianne Cahill hit the sauce more than ever, and Richie had to help Myron get her into the car for her driver to take her home.

Finally, Richie couldn't put it off any longer and went home. When he reached his house, relief filled him to see Rebecca's

SUV in the driveway. She had parked to one side so he could get his Porsche into the garage.

He couldn't wait to be with her in his house, in his bed.

He bounded up the stairs, got himself a glass of water, then made sure everything was locked up tight as he hurried to his bedroom.

It was empty.

Not even Spike was in there.

Then he understood. He couldn't help but inwardly chuckle at Rebecca. She was clearly in "virtuous daughter" mode with her mother being here. Earlier, she had made a big deal of telling Lorene she was putting Spike's bed in the guest bedroom that *she* was using—as if Lorene didn't know what was going on between the two of them. He always knew she had a bit of a puritanical streak, which was why he had put Lorene in the other end of the house. If he had a bedroom in the basement, he'd have gladly sent her down there.

Being with Lorene was beyond uncomfortable. She had questioned him about Big Caesar's and had made it clear she didn't find running a nightclub to be suitable employment. He couldn't help but wonder what she'd think about his other way of making money—the money that paid for this house, his other properties, and even his cars.

At times, he thought about giving up his other business, the one where he "fixed" things for people, except that it paid really well and gave him a lot of contacts and insights not available to most people. He knew better than to imagine his nightclub would be popular forever. Their lifespans were often short, and once word got out that a club was "so yesterday," it died a quick death.

But the rich and powerful always managed to get themselves into trouble, and being successful at helping them out of such jams was the kind of thing that caused a person's reputation to grow over time, not diminish. And the amount he could charge for services rendered grew accordingly.

And so, since he very much enjoyed his lifestyle, he was, in a word, stuck.

His biggest problem in all this was Rebecca.

He hung up his suit and took off his shirt, throwing it in the dirty clothes hamper, his mood going downhill as he thought about her troubles and how they mixed—or didn't mix well —with his.

Since meeting her, he'd tried more than ever to stay on the correct side of the law. In the past, he'd sometimes gotten so close to the line he might even have inadvertently crossed it. Nothing serious, but not good either. In Catholic terms, venial sins, not mortal ones.

Fortunately, he'd never been caught.

Now, though, thinking about Matteo Veltroni and the politicians he'd spent the evening with, he realized he might need to get close to that edge again. But it was for a good cause. It was to help Rebecca.

He wanted to spend time with her and not worry about the dangers surrounding her. That she hunted murderers was bad enough, but knowing people supposedly on her side could be targeting her made him crazy. If he didn't figure out what was happening soon, he would side with Lorene about Rebecca going back to Idaho until this trouble passed.

But who, he wanted to know, was this "Ed"? One thing was for sure: anyone who had dumped Rebecca was an idiot loser.

Barefoot, now wearing pajama bottoms, he tiptoed down the hall to Rebecca's room, quietly opened the door and peeked in. Hardly any moonlight came in through the window. He could barely see Spike curled up in his little bed, but then the dog's head rose. Realizing it was Richie, he quickly lay back down to sleep again. The faint light also let him see Rebecca in bed, bundled up with blankets.

He got under the covers, but as he turned toward her, he froze. What was that smell?

He inched closer. The scent reminded him of what Carmela called "cold cream," some goop she smeared on her face at night to fight wrinkles. Rebecca didn't have wrinkles ...

He felt as if ice water ran down his spine. He jumped out of bed so fast he all but levitated. Easing himself from the bed, he tiptoed backward until he was out of the room, then shut the door and ran down the hall to his bedroom. His heart pounded from the mistake—mistake, hell, catastrophic blunder—that he had almost made.

Just then he heard a light tap on his own bedroom door. His breath caught at the same time as a cold sweat struck his brow. Was that Lorene? Had he awoken her?

"Richie?" It was Rebecca's voice.

He flung open the door. "Where the hell were you?" he demanded.

She looked confused. "When?"

"Just now." His arms flapped against his sides. "Why is your mother in 'your' room?"

"Mom was afraid of being alone on the other side of the house, so I let her take it. I was on the sofa waiting up for you and must have fallen asleep. I thought I'd hear you when you got home. Why?"

"I went in there." He spoke through gritted teeth. "And I ... I *nearly* got into bed with her!" Some things, he decided, were better left unsaid.

As his words penetrated, her eyes widened. She began to snicker and finally fell into a full belly laugh.

"I'm glad you find it so hilarious," he said, his arms flailing about even more than usual.

She tried to be serious but she couldn't stop chuckling. "I'm sorry, but the look on your face…"

"You think this is funny?" He strode back and forth across the bedroom.

She laughed harder.

"She could have killed me! From shock if nothing else."

She tried to stop laughing, she really did, but whenever she looked at him she would start in again.

He put his hands on his hips. "Just the thought of … Oh, my God! I may never be able to get it up again!"

"I'm sure you'll be just fine." She wrapped her arms around him, stopping his pacing and gyrating, and made him face her. "I'm sorry. Really. And I shouldn't laugh."

Somewhat mollified, he folded his arms. "I'll probably have visions of Lorene next to me as soon as I shut my eyes."

She turned back the covers on his bed, and with great exaggeration, batted her eyelashes. "Can I help?"

He fought a smile. "I'm not sure."

She shrugged and sashayed toward the door. "Guess I'll just have to go back to the sofa to sleep."

He grabbed her hand, stopping her. "On second thought," he said, drawing her ever closer, his voice low and sultry, "maybe we should see what we can do about my potential problems with insomnia … and other delicate matters."

27

R ebecca didn't get much sleep that night, and it wasn't only because of Richie. About six a.m. her phone buzzed. She nearly knocked it off the nightstand in her rush to keep the ringing from waking Richie. Once firmly in her hand, she saw Eastwood's name, and answered immediately. He never called early. Unless there was good reason.

"Deputy Mayor Dianne Cahill's dead. Murdered."

Rebecca could barely breathe.

"You need to get to the crime scene now! I'm putting every detective on this one."

He gave her a minimum of detail, just the address. His words were rushed, but she'd learned all she needed to know for now.

It wasn't long before she'd uttered a quick "I've gotta run," to Richie and was out of the house.

She was shocked to find that the crime scene was only two blocks away from Daryl Hawley's home. Jared was already there, as were Paavo, Yosh, and Calderon. Bo Benson arrived minutes after her.

Eastwood was strutting around in front of a number of TV

cameras and crews, even as more were setting up. Rebecca guessed word of the death had gone out over police scanners.

It didn't take long for her to learn the details. A couple of patrol officers had spotted a Tesla in the Bayview-Hunters Point area with the front half up on the sidewalk and the back end jutting onto the street. They thought someone intoxicated had driven it up there, but when they checked on the driver, they found the deputy mayor slumped over the wheel. She had a bullet wound to the head.

Soon, Eastwood tore himself away from the press and gathered his detectives together. "I'm giving Paavo and Yosh the lead on this case, but every one of you needs to help wrap this up as soon as possible. One of the first questions we need answered is why was Cahill here? In fact, why was she out at all in the middle of the night? And why was she driving instead of using her driver? This is hardly a neighborhood for someone like her. Was she just passing through? If so, from where? To where?"

He continued. "I want Calderon, Bo, Rebecca, and Jared to canvass this entire neighborhood. Get a good handle on who may or may not have seen anything. I know it's what patrol cops usually do, but I want Homicide looking into every aspect of what happened here. I don't want to take the chance of missing something the first time through because some new officer didn't know the right questions to ask, or how to ask them. Understand?"

They all nodded, filled with the horror of what might end up being a political assassination in their city.

Richie had a leisurely routine when he got up each morning. He would start the day picking up the newspaper outside his front door and then continue to the kitchen to make a cup of strong Americano.

He'd look at the front page as the coffee brewed and then he'd go back to his bedroom where he would turn on his three televisions: one on an all-day business channel, another on a national news channel, and the third for local news and sports. He would place all on mute and then rely on news crawls to decide what, if anything, he needed to listen to while he sat on the bed to drink his coffee, read the paper, and check his phone for messages.

Eventually, he'd shower, dress, and determine how to spend his day between his nightclub and his "other" business duties.

But nothing was normal these days.

Very early that morning, he'd heard Rebecca's phone buzz. He'd guessed it was before dawn because the room was still dark, but he must have fallen right back to sleep because when he opened his eyes again, the sky was bright and he was left with the realization that he was alone in the house with Lorene.

Unfortunately, Lorene was still there. The last thing he wanted was to face her. Thank God she had slept through him in her room last night—at least he hoped she had. He shuddered whenever he thought of it.

So that morning, when he got out of bed, he tiptoed through the house, grabbed the newspaper, made his morning coffee, and fled back to his bedroom. He switched on the TVs and gawked in stunned silence at the breaking news: the death, an apparent murder, of Deputy Mayor Dianne Cahill.

Thoughts flooded over him of seeing her last evening, of her beauty and her heartache. And of how delicate she had seemed as they had danced. His emotions were conflicted. If she were behind the attacks on Rebecca, he should hate her. But at the same time, he was sorry about her death and sorry that all her promise had been so badly misguided.

He put down everything and was about to call Vito and Shay when his phone rang.

He couldn't believe who was calling: Myron Swain, Dianne Cahill's brother-in-law.

~

As Lt. Eastwood had ordered, Rebecca canvassed neighbors in the area where Dianne Cahill had been murdered. But as soon as she finished her assigned area, she drove to the grocer to ask if the milk-buying man had returned, or if the grocer had any thoughts about who he might be or where he might be found.

But, the grocer had nothing new to add.

Rebecca again drove through the neighborhood, even slowing down as she passed the creepy old mortuary. She wasn't usually squeamish about such places, but that one gave her a weird feeling. She had no idea why. Probably too many horror films as a youngster.

She soon left the area to return to Homicide. But she hadn't even reached her desk when Elizabeth stopped her and told her she was to immediately report to Lt. Eastwood.

Surprised, Rebecca knocked on the door and then entered his office.

"Have a seat," Eastwood said, not bothering to rise. Back to old times, Rebecca thought.

"What's this about?" she asked.

"I'm sorry to inform you that Commissioner Barcelli has requested that you be removed from the Dianne Cahill investigation."

Rebecca eyebrows rose. "Oh? It's not as if I'm really involved, but may I ask why?"

She saw Eastwood's Adam's apple bob. "It has to do with you potentially being involved in a lawsuit we expect Virginia Kirk to file against the department."

"Oh, for pity's sake!" Rebecca couldn't stop herself from

exclaiming. "I was wondering when you'd bring that up. If ever. I know it's the reason Bill Sutter retired. Too bad I'm not old enough to join him."

Eastwood ignored her sarcasm. "Virginia Kirk is alleging discrimination against her because of perceived sexual orientation."

"*Perceived* sexual orientation? That's a new one." Rebecca could feel her anger rising, but she did all she could to stay calm. "If anyone were to look over the case file or read the transcripts from the trial, they would see that nothing about anyone's sexual orientation was ever an issue. Besides, all charges against Virginia Kirk were dropped."

"But you continue to believe she was guilty."

"I do."

"That, in itself, Ginny Kirk's lawyer will say, demonstrates your bias against her."

Rebecca's eyes narrowed. "And because of this potential lawsuit, I can't work on a case?"

"Correct."

"No." Rebecca's word was filled with defiance. "It has to do with my other investigations. Someone's been after me because they're afraid of where those investigations might lead. You know it, *sir*. And so do I."

"You're jumping to conclusions, Rebecca."

"Am I? I know Virginia Kirk and Dianne Cahill were friends. And everyone knows Commissioner Barcelli was nothing but a puppet for Dianne Cahill. Even with her dead, he still doesn't want me involved! What's he afraid I'll find out? Maybe I'll turn up something incriminating not only her, but him as well."

"Rebecca, enough!" Eastwood roared. "You have no proof of what you're saying. I suggest you forget that entire line of thinking."

"Virginia Kirk isn't the problem for me or this department." She stood and folded her arms. "The commissioner is."

"One more word, Mayfield, and you're suspended."

The man didn't even have the decency to look embarrassed. "Yes, sir. Tell me this, will the commissioner allow me to continue to work on the Paula Forsyth and Daryl Hawley murders as well as trying to find his missing kids?"

"You can work on the murders," Eastwood said. "But stay away from City Hall. Have Jared look into it."

"Jared? But–"

He held up his hand, stopping her. "You need to go back to your desk. Now."

Rebecca did as told, but she was furious. At least she hadn't been suspended and sent home.

She was contemplating the unfairness of the police commissioner getting involved in her working a homicide investigation when she received a call from her landlord, Bradley Frick.

"What's going on, Rebecca?" he asked. "There's a crowd outside my flat looking for you. I went out there and told them you didn't live here, but they seem to know you do. They're screaming that you're homophobic."

She put a hand to her forehead and tried to explain the situation to him, but Bradley interrupted. He was a man plagued with nervousness and the crowd outside had all but pushed him over the edge. "They're loud and disruptive and brought the police into our little street. Not only that, they're towing cars that are parked on top of the red zone! Do you know how much our neighbors are going to hate me? And you?"

"I'm so sorry, Bradley. You can tell the demonstrators and the neighbors that I *used* to live on Mulford, but I've moved. How's that? I'm staying elsewhere. Spike is with me. We won't be back until this is over."

"I hope so," he said. "I like you, you know that, but I can't let one of my tenants disrupt the entire neighborhood this way. And if this is a court case, it'll take forever before anything is resolved."

"I know," she murmured, hating what was happening as much as he did. She loved her little apartment, her private yard. It wasn't much, but it was hers. It was one thing to leave because she preferred living elsewhere, such as with Richie. It was quite another to be forced out.

She guessed Bradley would ask her to move if this went on much longer. "Tell me, do you have any idea how they even know what's going on? So far, no lawsuit has been filed."

"It's in today's *Chronicle*. And the news report is very one-sided, I'm sorry to say."

She should have known. "All I can tell you is that the charges against me are untrue. I believe the woman I arrested is guilty of murder. She's suing the city and me based on a false narrative."

"I see," he said, somewhat mollified. "So, where are you going?"

"It's best if I don't say. That way, you'll be able to tell people you don't know."

"It's probably your Porsche-driving boyfriend's house," he murmured.

"But then," she said, "I'd be putting him in a similar situation to the one you're in."

"That's true," he mused. "Guess that means I really don't know where you're hiding out. Thanks for doing this, Rebecca. I know it can't be easy."

"It's damned hard," she said honestly.

She no sooner hung up the phone than she saw her mother approaching her desk. *Now what?*

"I didn't want to interrupt your phone call," Lorene said.

"Why are you here?" Rebecca asked, her mind going through

all kinds of terrible scenarios that might have brought her mother to Homicide. "Is something wrong?"

"Yes, something is very wrong," she announced. "I read an article in the newspaper about you being sued by some woman you arrested for murder!"

Rebecca groaned. She should have known.

"Of course, I don't believe it. But I don't understand how you can put up with these crazy people attacking your character with no good reason. I know you aren't prejudiced against these LGB ... whatever people. But I'm worried about you! I swear, Rebecca, what more can happen in this God-forsaken city with this dangerous job? You need to come home with me. *Now!*"

Rebecca sighed. She couldn't help but wonder if her mother was right.

28

Myron Swain was sitting at a table at Bar Nua, an old-fashioned Irish pub in a sea of Italian establishments on Columbus Avenue, when Richie arrived. The room was relatively dark with wooden tables, lots of benches and stools, some booths, and a long bar where customers could eye a huge selection of hard liquor and ales. TV screens with sports played non-stop over the bar area.

Richie sat at the table, ordered a Guinness, and waited for Myron to explain why he had called. It didn't take long.

"I'm in a fix," Myron said. The guy was so scared, he kept looking over his shoulder even though he was sitting with a wall behind him. "I, uh, had the impression from our meeting last night, that you, uh, help people."

"Sometimes," Richie said calmly. "It depends on the problem. So, you need to tell me what's wrong."

Myron's left eye twitched badly. "Talking to you is sort of like talking to a lawyer, right? I mean, there's client-lawyer privilege, so you can't go blabbing to the police, right?"

"I'm no attorney and don't pretend to be," Richie said. "That said, if I went around telling others my clients' secrets, I wouldn't be in business very long, would I?"

"No, I guess not."

"And you wouldn't be here if my reputation for doing good work wasn't solid, am I right?" Richie asked.

"Actually, it's because Matteo Veltroni likes you."

This guy, Richie thought, really was a jerk. "Well, then, what's your worry?"

Myron chewed his bottom lip. "It's just that it's difficult.... What we did, what I did, working for Dianne ... some of it ... some of it was stupid. It made us rich, but we should have been more careful. But I ... we ... never expected." He gave a trembling sigh. "I can't believe she's gone."

"Do you know who killed her?" he asked softly.

"No, not at all." Myron gulped some beer. "All I can say is with Dianne dead, I wonder if any of it was worth it."

Myron's words weren't making much sense, but the guy looked ready to crack.

"Maybe we can work things out and set them right." Richie's tone became soothing, even velvety. "Or, at a minimum, make them much less hard on you. Can we try that?"

Myron nodded.

"Good. Now, you need to start at the beginning."

Myron licked his lips.

Richie gave an encouraging nod.

"We have a deal, then?" Myron asked.

"Sure. Why not?" Richie said with a smile. Suddenly he felt something jabbing into his thigh. What the hell? Was the little twerp getting fresh? He reached down to grab a couple of fingers and twist hard, but instead felt a thick letter-size envelope.

He understood. If it wasn't filled with ones, it was a lot. Amateurs, he thought. He took the envelope and without glancing at it, tucked it into his jacket's inside breast pocket. "You can start anytime."

Myron's eyes suddenly turned a little hopeful. "Okay." He gave a small cough. "Some time back, almost three years, Dianne was dating a doctor who was, I'm sorry to say, a coke-head. He was burning through his money at a fast clip and needed some way to find more. Earlier, he had contracted with the city to help care for homeless patients. He often prescribed an anti-depressant called Lulz which the city was getting at a good price from the company's new owner."

Richie nodded. The infamous Lulz.

"Needless to say, the discount eventually ended. The company, Blaxor, tried to say the drug's high cost was worth paying because of its lack of side effects. At the same time, a new study cast doubt on the drug's effectiveness. Most doctors dropped it, but Dianne's friend continued to prescribe it and billed the city for reimbursement. When no one questioned him about the expense, the doctor set up a system where he wrote prescriptions he never actually filled. And continued to bill the city for the drugs he never dispensed, drugs he apparently never even ordered."

"I see," Richie murmured. "And he pocketed the money?"

"You got it," Myron said. "One day I was looking over a report on monies the city was paying to care for our indigent population and noticed what seemed to be an excessive amount going to one clinic. I knew Dianne was dating a doctor there and told her about it. She said she'd check it out."

As Richie waited, Myron again sipped some beer, his mouth seeming to grow drier by the minute. "When Dianne learned what the doctor was doing, she quit dating him."

"How much money are we talking about?" Richie asked.

Myron grimaced. "That one doctor bought in a grand each day."

"One grand? For doing nothing?" Richie asked, beginning to think he was in the wrong line of work.

"Right. As Dianne told me about it, we realized that on a larger scale the process could bring in a ton of money. Money is the mother's milk of politics and power, not to mention all the goodies that make life so much easier."

Myron continued. "We looked into the company, Blaxor, and Dianne got to know the company's owner. Varg Hague is a Norwegian entrepreneur who got rich buying and selling companies. He hired an American, Paula Forsyth, as his vice president. It was clear their only interest in the company was to make money off it, whatever it took. Also, the two were having an affair, despite both being married at that time."

Richie's eyebrows rose. "And then?"

"To our surprise, when Dianne explained our little plan to make some extra money off Lulz, Hague and Forsyth agreed. We got them at the right time. It's easy to persuade people with cash flow problems and debt coming due. We, I mean *Dianne*, didn't even have to blackmail them about their affair."

Richie thought his regard for Myron Swain couldn't sink any lower than it already had. He'd been wrong. "How did it work?"

"We set up a system where fake purchase orders from the city went directly to Forsyth for approval and were kept off Blaxor's real books. The city continued to do some legitimate Blaxor purchases to help mask these others."

"So they executed the plan?" Richie asked.

"Yes, and for a couple of years everyone was happy. We did it small scale, not enough to bring any unwanted attention."

"What happened?"

"For a long time, all was quiet. Dianne met and fell for Clive Hutchinson, as I'm sure you noticed. He was an analyst in the accounting branch. He's also ambitious and realized how important she could be to his career. But he had nothing. No money and lots of student loans. Dianne soon got him a promotion to the head of the Department of Management and Budget. The boy needed money big time to live life as he wanted, and so we eased him into our real estate scheme."

"You mean your money laundering plan," Richie interrupted.

"Such an ugly term for intelligent fiscal management," Myron said. "Anyway, some people died, and eventually, it got too hot to continue, so we pulled the plug. Collateral damage draws too much unwanted attention."

Suddenly, Richie felt his head grow light. Then the room began to spin as the realization struck that he was sitting face-to-face with the man who was the brains behind the real estate and other illegal schemes Rebecca had been working on and upending the past few months ... that this was the man who had started it all, years back ... years before Richie had even met Rebecca ... back when he was younger and a less cynical, world-weary person, when he had a fiancée and planned to marry, to raise a family. His fiancée had died because of one of Myron Swain's schemes. Recently, with Richie's help, Rebecca had worked the cold case that resulted in some bank executives and a few others who were involved in the death being put behind bars.

But they hadn't been able to find the source of the illegal activities.

All they knew was that the source was very likely someone in City Hall.

And now, here he was.

And he had the nerve to call the deaths he'd caused, the lives he'd destroyed, "collateral damage." How easily he had said "some people died." But they weren't "some people." They had names, and one of those names was Isabella.

Her death had all but destroyed Richie. It had taken a lot of years, and a lot of support from Shay and Vito for him to ever get over her loss. And only recently, since getting to know Rebecca, did he begin to even think about the future.

It was all he could do to stop himself from grabbing the man before him—that complete and total bastard—and after wiping the smirk off his face, bashing his head in.

He didn't move a muscle, but as he stared at Myron, he vowed to get even.

Unfazed, Myron sipped his beer and continued. "The problem was, we soon realized the Lulz scheme wasn't big enough to support all of us and Clive without the real estate money. We all had expenses, and we had to do something. So we increased the fake sales of Lulz. A lot. Hague and Forsyth didn't like it, but they had no choice. We needed the money."

"Had someone caught on by then?" Richie asked.

"No. We were still in the clear. The only 'issue' that came up was when Clive was promoted to the mayor's chief of staff position. Once that happened, he wanted out of anything to do with Blaxor. He was all about ambition, following Warren to Sacramento, and maybe eventually to the White House. Clive also wanted to be rid of Dianne. There were aspects to her that could be a liability. By the way, the woman you saw him with is not only beautiful but she's from the Turpin family, one of San Francisco's oldest and richest. If he snags her, she could easily finance his personal ambition."

Richie was trying to understand the big picture. "Are you saying you think Clive Hutchinson is behind the murders? That he had to get rid of Forsyth and Cahill because they knew about his involvement? If so, Varg Hague is in danger, as you are. Is that it?"

"I don't know," Myron admitted. "For all his ambition, I don't see Clive as a killer, but if not him, who? That's why I'm scared. I need to free myself from this whole ugly situation. Take the money, stay safe, and wait for another day."

"Is anyone else involved in this plan besides you, Dianne, Clive, and the two Blaxor lovers?"

Myron blanched. "Not that I know of. But you never know who smells easy money and joins the feeding frenzy."

Richie felt stymied. "One last question. Virginia Kirk. What does she have to do with any of this?"

"Oh, her. She used to work for city government. In the accounting department with Clive Hutchinson, in fact." A cloud seemed to cross Myron's face, and he studied the tabletop a moment. "Dianne was a first-class manipulator. Truly gifted. She knew how to make whoever she was with think she was wonderful and also needed to be protected, as if she were some fragile creature that relied on their help."

Richie swallowed hard, realizing that was exactly what had happened to him.

Myron finished his beer. "I never knew exactly what happened, but some years back, a woman named Sharon Lynch was sticking her nose in where it didn't belong about the Lulz drug. Sharon was a social worker and saw that the drug did little good. In fact, she thought it did nothing but keep its users down and out. She hated Lulz and told her roommate, Virginia Kirk, who mentioned it to Dianne. That put Dianne on alert. Also, Dianne knew Kirk wanted Sharon out of her apartment and her life. She encouraged Virginia to get Sharon out of *both* their lives. Virginia did—but she also had a built-in insurance policy to assure that she didn't end up in jail. If things went south for her, she could implicate Dianne in the Blaxor scam and put her reputation and political life at risk."

"You're kidding me." Richie hadn't seen that coming.

"Not at all. By this time, Sharon was nothing more than another irritant to be neutralized." For the first time, Myron smiled, obviously enjoying being the person who knew others' secrets. "Supposedly, at the time of Sharon's murder, Virginia was out of the state—the perfect alibi. But when some nosy cop named, uh, Rebecca Mayfield got the case, she didn't accept the theory that some mysterious stranger had broken into the apartment and killed Sharon. Mayfield and her partner wanted to charge Virginia Kirk with murder one. Kirk was beside herself. Dianne got her off by pushing public sympathy for Kirk and finding the—*ahem*—evidence that got her released."

"Finding or creating evidence?" Richie asked.

Myron shrugged, again with a hint of a smile on his face.

The thought of these people hurting Rebecca's case and her reputation infuriated Richie. He knew all too well how hard she worked and how important she believed her job to be. These people had attacked the two women he loved and must be brought to judgment—the law's or his.

"What about now?" Richie asked. "Was Dianne the one pushing Kirk to sue the police department?"

"Oh, you know about the lawsuit?" Myron actually looked impressed. "Well, when Dianne learned that Mayfield was now looking into corruption in city government, she decided Virginia Kirk was a good way to get rid of her. It took a while, but finally we located Kirk, and Dianne talked her into threatening to file the lawsuit. Dianne could be very persuasive."

Richie hated to ask the obvious question, but he had to. His mouth went dry as he said, "Why didn't Dianne Cahill simply put out a contract on the cop, this Rebecca Mayfield? Why not just shoot her in the back and get it over with?"

Myron looked horrified. "Dianne was no killer. It was a step too far for her. Whatever you might think about her, she was a decent person. Even if she played a role in the overall money-making scheme, she was no killer. An unwitting accomplice after the fact at worst. It ate her up.

"In fact, she was quite angry when someone in the police commission or department or wherever (which, of course, I don't know about) apparently paid someone to do a hit job on Rebecca, even as recently as this week. They shot and missed, which might have been a good thing. If Rebecca had been murdered in cold blood, her colleagues would have started looking into her cases in depth. No, it either had to look like an on-the-job fatality, or Dianne needed to get rid of her by some other means, like the Kirk lawsuit."

Richie forced himself to remain still, not to speak, not to move … or he might have reached over and strangled the fish-faced little snot on the spot. Finally, his emotions somewhat under control, he said, "You need to get Kirk to call off her lawsuit."

"I don't know—"

"Do you want my help or not?"

Myron thought a moment. "Okay. I'll get her to stop. Hell, without Dianne pushing her, Kirk will probably be happy to go back into hiding."

Disappear completely and forever would be best, Richie mused. He stood, tossed a twenty on the table and walked out of the restaurant, leaving Myron sitting alone and probably wondering what Richie would do to help him out of his mess.

Help him? Yeah, he'd help him all right. He'd help him pay for all he did—one way or another.

29

R ichie, Vito, and Shay met in their usual private booth at the Leaning Tower Taverna. Richie filled them in on his meeting with Myron Swain.

"It's time we talk to Varg Hague," Richie said. "Everything Myron told me implicated him in these schemes, but I have no proof against him. If he denied he ever said those things, it would be his word against mine. Hague, on the other hand, should tell us the truth. He has to realize he could well be next on the killer's hit list."

"Unless Hague is the killer," Shay said. "We seem to be running low on suspects."

"My number one suspect is dead," Richie muttered. "I was sure Dianne Cahill was the one behind them, but then she ended up a victim."

Richie took a quick swallow of beer and looked at Vito. "Do you have a burner phone on you?"

Vito pulled one out of the pocket of his oversized, well-worn jacket and handed it to Richie. The man always kept a supply of burners handy. Richie never wanted to think of what else might be inside that jacket.

Without Richie needing to ask, Shay took a napkin and jotted down Varg Hague's personal cell phone number, and Richie put in a call to the Blaxor director. "We need to talk," he said, putting the phone on speaker.

"Who is this?" Hague asked.

"You don't know me, but I know all about you. You're in danger and I can help. I'll be at the spot where you and Paula Forsyth met Dianne Cahill on Tuesday morning."

"I won't do it. Who the hell are you?"

"As I said, I'm trying to help. You must realize whoever killed Forsyth and Cahill has his sights on you, as well. I'll see you in one hour."

He hung up the phone and joined Vito and Shay in high fives

Richie, Vito and Shay drove separate cars to the mortuary. They went there immediately after Richie ended the call, arriving a half-hour early. Richie parked near the back lot's driveway while Vito and Shay got into position to cover him in case Hague went cowboy and tried to take him out. They couldn't forget that Hague might be behind Forsyth and Cahill's deaths.

But even if he was, Richie doubted Varg Hague would have acted on his own. Executives never liked to dirty their own hands. Richie had no idea just how big the conspiracy was, or how many people Hague might have helping him.

The time for Hague to meet him came and went. A half hour later, Richie got out of his car and went to the back of the mortuary. It was empty and, appropriately, silent as a tomb.

Soon, Vito and Shay joined him. "I guess we did too good a job scaring him," Richie said. "He may have done a runner."

"Where to now, boss?" Vito asked.

"Vito, why don't you go to his apartment, see if you can find him there," Richie said, then turned toward Shay. "You can see if he's still at work."

"I will, but first I've got to pick up Hannah. I promised I'd meet her after school. She's had it a little rough lately."

"No problem," Richie said. "The poor kid has been through a lot. I think I'll check in with Rebecca. See if she's turned up leads on Dianne Cahill's murder. That might help explain some of this. And, that reminds me. Rebecca has a new partner, Jared Woolridge, formerly with the police department's Legal Division. I'd like you to find out all you can about him."

"Sure thing. I'll add it to my ever-growing list."

Richie had no sympathy, and said only, "Good."

As they walked back toward their cars, Shay stopped at the mortuary's side door and rattled it, then tried the window. Both were locked. "There's something weird about this place."

"Maybe there's something about the ownership of it," Richie said.

"I already looked into that. The city owns it now, but there could be something interesting inside. The city might not have even bothered to check it out," Shay said, then glanced at his watch. "I'll come back later tonight."

"If you do, bring Vito with you," Richie said as he and Vito continued to walk toward their cars. "This place gives me the creeps."

Shay checked out a few more windows, tried to peer inside the building, but it looked dark and empty. He had the oddest feeling that neither man nor beast should ever enter the derelict building, but that feeling only provoked his curiosity. He would be back, sooner rather than later.

30

R ichie was sitting in Rebecca's chair in Homicide when she entered the bureau. He had pushed the chair over to Jared Woolridge's desk so he could get to know the guy. They'd talked about ten minutes, plenty long enough for Richie to decide he didn't like him.

Rebecca was scowling as she approached him. "What are you doing here?"

"Waiting for you." He couldn't help but smile at her frown.

She turned to Jared. "So, you two have met."

"Sure did," Jared said, arms folded. "Now I know what a suspect feels like when questioned."

"I wasn't that bad," Richie said somewhat sheepishly. He rolled Rebecca's chair back in place and faced her. "But I'm here for a reason. Do you have time for coffee?"

She understood he wanted to talk privately. "Sure."

Richie and Jared said quick goodbyes.

"He seems to be an interesting guy," Richie said, studying Rebecca carefully as they waited for the elevator down to the cafeteria. "Handsome, too."

"Is he?" Rebecca asked coyly. "I hadn't noticed."

"Hah!"

She grinned.

Once they were seated with lattes, Richie asked, "Did you ever hear anything about Woolridge before his reassignment?" He hoped he sounded unbiased and simply curious.

"You've really got a thing for him, don't you?" she said with a grin.

He guessed he'd failed the unbiased part. "I told you I thought he was cute. But I'm serious. What do you think of him getting Bill Sutter's job?"

She sipped her latte. "That's the thing. There are a lot of men and women in the SFPD who've been waiting a long time for an opening in Homicide. They've got fabulous marks on their tests and outstanding recommendations from their superiors, yet the top brass suddenly pulls in a guy no one has ever heard of, from an admin job no less, and that makes no sense. I called a woman in admin that I know fairly well, and she hasn't even called me back. Luis Calderon is trying to find out what's going on from some of his sources, too, but so far no one is talking. I can't help but wonder if his reassignment has to do with the lawsuit Virginia Kirk is threatening to bring against me. For all I know, he might have been sent here to spy on me."

"Since he got the transfer the same night Bill Sutter resigned, it's suspicious," Richie said. He was tempted to tell her the Kirk lawsuit would most likely be dropped, but he needed to wait until he was sure Myron had squashed it. Instead, he changed subjects. "I'm wondering what's going on with Dianne Cahill's murder investigation. Any luck so far?"

Rebecca's lips curled in disgust. "It's not my case. Eastwood gave the lead to Paavo and Yosh, as if it's too 'high profile' for me and a rookie. I heard she received a text that got her to the scene, but it was from a burner phone. I have no details as yet."

"Damn. I was hoping that could clarify some very loose ends."

"What do you mean?"

He told her about his meeting with Myron Swain. "Bottom line," he said finally, "Cahill was the one who got Virginia Kirk off after you figured out she had killed Sharon Lynch. Then, Cahill had a sweet deal going with real estate holding companies until you turned that upside down. After that, she tried to increase her income in the Blaxor drug scheme but Daryl Hawley was shot and you—again, you—discovered a connection to Blaxor."

"So I was like Banquo's ghost," Rebecca said. "Wherever she looked, I popped up to remind her of all she was doing that was wrong."

"Exactly. I can't help but suspect the thing that scared Cahill the most was that you might turn up her involvement in Sharon Lynch's murder case, but even the embezzlement and money-laundering with the real estate and drug schemes would lead to jail time. I'm sure that was the reason for the attacks on you, and the Virginia Kirk lawsuit. She wanted to get rid of you one way or the other."

Rebecca tilted her head. "But if so, if Dianne Cahill was behind all that, why was she killed?"

"That, my dear inspector, is the million dollar question," Richie said. "It also means that, even though Cahill is dead, others who worked both with her and against her—including you and me —may still be in danger."

31

A fter leaving Richie, Rebecca couldn't stop thinking about Virginia Kirk's case. Something bothered her. She couldn't remember Dianne Cahill being involved at all. Instead of returning to Homicide, she went to the case file storage lockers and asked for the box of records on the Sharon Lynch murder.

As she went through the files, one thing jumped out at her that hadn't been an issue during the time of the investigation and trial. Sharon Lynch had worked as an aide under a program established by the San Francisco Community Clinic Consortium to provide comprehensive care for the homeless. She mostly worked at a clinic in the Haight-Ashbury, although she also served numerous other locations.

One of her many assignments was to make sure the medical sections of the clinics were well stocked with drugs, bandages, and those medicines the doctors commonly prescribed to their patients.

Rebecca looked at the places Lynch worked and then picked up the list she had gotten from RX Wholesale of the places where Daryl Hawley made his deliveries. A number of clinics were on both.

She phoned Hawley's boss at RX Wholesale and asked him to check his records to see if Hawley had a route three years earlier that included the same clinics. After much complaining about her question, the boss let her know that Hawley did have the route.

Since both Hawley and Lynch had a hand in medical supply deliveries and disbursements, there was a distinct possibility they knew each other.

And now both were dead … three years apart.

She could find nothing in the Lynch files about Daryl Hawley.

As Shay waited for Hannah's school to let out, he wondered how tough Hannah's persecutors really were. It was one thing for them to pick on the girl when a sweet woman like Mrs. Brannigan was there to meet her, but he was sure they'd sing a different tune after he spoke to them.

He didn't like being crude, but he hoped the little bastards would piss their pants when they saw him and understood what might happen to them if they kept up their bullying.

He also suspected Hannah wouldn't tell him who her tormenters were, so as the kids poured out of the building, he stood out of sight in a doorway across the street. He saw Hannah emerge and then, as she had been instructed, she remained inside the school gates waiting to be picked up.

Two boys swaggered up to her. The belligerent way they stood made Shay certain they were mouthing off. Hannah looked upset, and Shay's anger flashed. When one boy pushed her shoulder and made her stumble back a few steps, Shay had seen enough.

In quick strides, he stood before them. His voice was both soft and deadly as he said, "You two will apologize to Hannah and never speak that way to her again."

The two boys looked at each other. One that Shay guessed

was the stupider of the two raised his chin. "You aren't the boss of me!"

Shay wanted to laugh in his face. Instead, he simply smiled, having been told that his smile was more chilling than most people's frowns. The boys had the good sense to shift nervously.

His voice turned even softer as he murmured, "No, I'm not. It's up to you to decide how you will treat Hannah. But I suggest you think about it very, very carefully." He then let his grin broaden.

Terrified, the two boys stumbled backward.

"Go home," Shay said. "I'll be watching."

They ran from the school.

Hannah looked up at him. "You scared them, Shay."

"If they bother you again, I'll do more than that."

"I don't think they will." She sounded a little scared of him as well. He hated that.

He smoothed his ascot, then placed his slim hand on her narrow shoulder. "Why don't we go get an ice cream? Would you like that?"

"With sprinkles?" she asked.

"Even dipped in chocolate, if you'd like."

"I'd like."

The ice cream shop was only three blocks away, the weather was beautiful, so they decided to walk.

Hannah was playing her own version of hopscotch with lines on the sidewalk. She ran ahead of him, to show him how she could hop and not land on a line, then she turned and faced him. "How was that?" she asked.

He smiled—a genuine, from the heart smile. "You did great."

Suddenly, her expression changed as she looked past him, then pointed. "*Daddy!*"

He spun around to see where she was looking. At the site of a gun pointed at them, he lunged at Hannah, pushing her onto the street between two parked cars as a shot rang out.

He glanced at Hannah's frightened face, saw she was unharmed, took the Sig Sauer he always carried, and stepped back onto the sidewalk to look for the shooter. Whoever it had been, now seemed to have gone.

Only then did he feel the sharp pain in his back, near his shoulder blade. And then his legs gave out from under him.

32

Richie paced the hospital floor, checking his watch every few seconds, wondering why surgery was taking so long. Wondering if he had put Shay in harm's way.

The cops had told him that people in the neighborhood heard a gunshot and a child's cries, rushed onto the street to help, and someone called 911.

He stopped pacing when a woman in scrubs walked by, but she kept on walking. He sighed. God, he needed to know what was happening.

It was Hannah who'd called him, Hannah who told him, through tears that made her voice quiver, that Shay had been shot in the back, that he was covered with blood. He'd heard Shay's voice in the background, gasping for air. "Take care of Hannah. Please," he'd begged Richie, before a paramedic or cop or someone had taken the phone and after a few questions, told Richie which hospital Shay was being transported to, and that the little girl would be there, waiting to be turned over to his care.

It was clear from Shay's voice, his words, that something about his daughter was worrying him even more than having been shot.

Richie had rushed to the hospital. There, he found Hannah by the nurse's station.

She hugged him. Tears streaked her face. Richie tried to calm her as much as he could.

Holding Hannah's hand tightly, he went to the nurse's station and asked, "How is Henry Tate?"

"Are you a relative?" yet another woman in green scrubs asked.

"Yes." He lied. "A cousin."

"He's still in surgery."

"How bad is he?"

"The doctor will let you know his condition when surgery's over. But … apparently, Mr. Tate refused to be put under, so they're using a local on him." Typical for Shay. He could never do things the easy way. "I'm sure he'll be out of surgery soon. When he's out of recovery, you and his daughter will be able to meet with him.."

He squeezed Hannah's hand tighter. Tears had dried on her face and somehow she offered him a weak smile. He was sure his own smile was equally weak.

He'd bought her a cup of hot chocolate and a pack of cookies from the vending machines, then found a comfortable place to sit, a place quiet enough for him to call Rebecca.

And then he'd begun to pace. Waiting impatiently.

Before long, Rebecca rushed into the surgery waiting room. "How is he?" she asked, when Richie took her shoulders. He told her as much as he knew about his condition, which wasn't much.

"Do you know what happened?" she asked.

"Not yet. I spoke to him only briefly, just long enough for him to make it clear he wanted me to stay with Hannah until he could talk."

Rebecca frowned, her expression telling him she was as confused by that as he was.

And then the three of them waited together.

Rebecca found a *Highlights* magazine and worked a couple of puzzles with Hannah. Richie called Shay's housekeeper to fill her in on the little he knew. Somehow he convinced her that she didn't need to come to the hospital, that he'd keep Hannah close, and not to worry. He knew she would, but he'd promised Shay he'd take care of Hannah, and that meant he wouldn't hand her over into the care of *anyone*.

Next he called Vito. Before he could say anything other than Shay's been shot and mentioned the hospital, Vito hung up. He knew the man would knock down hell's gates to get there.

At long last, with Hannah's hand tucked tightly in Richie's, a nurse led them to a private recovery room where Shay would remain until stabilized. He was hooked up to an IV, but Richie knew that would be pulled out soon. The doctor had already told Richie that Shay was lucky, that the bullet had missed major arteries and hadn't hit any vital organs. He wanted to keep him overnight, but Shay had stated emphatically that he would not stay any longer than absolutely necessary, definitely not overnight, and insisted on being released as soon as possible.

That was exactly what Richie had expected.

When they walked up to the bed, Richie was stunned by what he saw. Shay was always pale, but he looked whiter than ever against the hospital sheets. Seeing him like that made Richie realize how much he cared about his strange friend.

He took a moment to find his voice. "That was a hell of a way to get attention," he said, managing to somehow find the ability to smile.

"That's me all right," Shay deadpanned, before his gaze moved from Richie and to Rebecca. "Where's Hannah?"

The little girl ducked out from behind Richie and moved close to the bed.

Shay smiled softly, somehow reaching out to caress Hannah's

cheek. He let her know in no uncertain terms that he was going to be okay and thanked her for calling Richie. Sentiment wasn't something Richie was used to seeing in his friend, but it was full-on when he spoke to his little girl.

He drew his hand and arm back to his side, winced, as if the movement caused a great deal of pain, and after thanking Richie for keeping Hannah close, he faced Rebecca. "Did the police get the gunman or find any leads?"

"Nothing yet," she said, hating to admit it. "I've put some calls in. Hopefully I'll learn something soon. Did you see the shooter?"

He shook his head slightly. "Not really, it happened too fast. I turned, saw a male, a gray hoodie pulled low covering most of his face, and a large caliber handgun. I immediately realized Hannah could be in the line of fire and all I could think of was to get her out of the way. But I may know who was behind it."

"You do?" Rebecca asked.

He nodded, his mouth a straight, fierce line. "Hannah saw the gunman. It was her calling out that saved me, maybe both of us." He shut his eyes, unable to stop the shudder that hit him at those words.

He looked at his daughter, studying her a moment. "I heard you say 'Daddy,'" he said softly to her. "Did you see Gebran Najjar? Is he the one who had the gun?"

She looked at him with surprise, then shook her head. "No."

"No? Then why did you say his name?"

"I wasn't talking about him," she said, then dropped her gaze and her voice grew very soft. "That's what I call you in my head. When I was scared, it just came out."

Shay's face remained emotionless for only a moment before Richie saw his every feature soften. Shay once again moved his arm from the bed, reaching out to touch the little girl's cheek, her head, her shoulder. "You can call me that instead of Shay any time you'd like. Okay?"

She nodded, beaming, and threw her arms around him, before easing up and holding him gently.

Shay kept an arm around Hannah as he again faced Richie. "They'll let me out of here soon. But if it wasn't Najjar who shot me ..."

Richie met his eyes and nodded.

Rebecca said, "I saw a kid-size table with color crayons as we walked in. Maybe Hannah would like to sit there and draw while we talk?"

Shay offered Hannah a questioning look. "Is that okay with you?"

It took a moment of intense concentration, before Hannah said, "I don't want to leave you. Can I just sit in the corner? I promise I won't listen."

Shay couldn't help but smile. "Sure, sweetheart."

It wasn't the best solution, Richie thought, but they couldn't have her sit alone in the waiting room, not now.

"I'll get some crayons. Be back in a moment," Rebecca said, and very soon, Hannah was sitting on the floor, crowded in by all sorts of medical equipment, but looking comfortable with the crayons. Rebecca hadn't found any coloring books, but pulled a few pieces of paper out of her purse, extra sketches of the man the grocer had identified, the man who might very well have been Hawley's shooter. "You can draw on these," she said. "I have lots of them."

"I don't know what to draw," Hannah whispered.

"Why don't you draw your Daddy?"

At those words, the girl smiled and picked up a yellow crayon.

As Rebecca rejoined Richie at Shay's bedside, Vito entered the room. He'd probably lied about his relationship to Shay, too.

No way would they be able to keep him out of the room. His distraught eyes stared a long moment at Shay.

"'Eh, *paisan*," Vito said. "What's this?"

"Just wanted to make sure you aren't taking me for granted," Shay said.

"Well, knock it off." Vito's face slowly formed a sad smile. "I've got things to do. I don't have time to worry about you!"

"Right. He's keeping us both too busy," Shay said with a nod toward Richie.

After a few jokes about Richie-as-boss, and then Richie and Shay needing to convince Vito that Shay would be all right, Rebecca interrupted the banter. "I know the three of you tried to meet Varg Hague," she said in hushed tones, so Hannah would have trouble hearing. "Do you think contacting him might have led to the attack on Shay?"

Richie, Vito and Shay eyed each other in the way of old friends who didn't need words to communicate. Finally, Richie answered. "We don't see how it could be. Anything's possible, of course, but we think Hague's gone into hiding."

"I went to his apartment," Vito said. "He wasn't home, which was hardly a surprise."

Rebecca nodded. "It sounds as if I need to look for Varg Hague. My new partner was supposed to question him and others at Blaxor after Paula Forsyth's murder, but I haven't heard any results from his meetings." She pulled out her cell phone. "Let me call."

Her conversation lasted less than a minute. "Jared hasn't been able to find Hague, and Hague hasn't returned his calls."

"That reminds me," Shay said. "I had a little time to look into Jared Woolridge's cell phone calls and texts. He met Dianne Cahill before going to work yesterday. And then, last night, someone killed her. I don't know if there's a connection or if it's all coincidence. Something fails the smell test."

Richie turned to Rebecca. "I can't imagine why someone in Woolridge's position would meet with a deputy mayor, can you?"

"No." Rebecca's brows crossed. "He didn't mention it to me, either. I'll see what I can find out."

"Be careful around him," Richie said. "I don't trust him."

"I'm sure Dianne Cahill met with a lot of people the day of her death," Rebecca mused. "There could be a perfectly logical reason for Jared to have seen her."

Richie was ready to offer a few more opinions about "Jared" when Hannah got up from the floor and walked over to Shay's bed. She was holding the papers she had been coloring on.

"I think someone wants to show you the drawing she made of you," Rebecca said to Shay, her gaze warm as she looked at Hannah.

"No," Hannah said, shaking her head. "I mean, yes. I'm making a drawing, but ..." Troubled eyes met Shay's.

"What is it?" he asked.

She handed him the paper with the artist's sketch. "That's the man who shot you."

Stunned, he took the paper, looking from it to Rebecca.

"My God," Rebecca said. "That's the man I suspect may have kidnapped Daryl Hawley's children."

Shay stiffened. He looked at Hannah, frowning. "You're sure this is the man you saw shoot me?"

"Yes." Hannah nodded. "I saw him before that, too.."

Shay's frown deepened.. "What do you mean? Where did you see him? When?"

"Yesterday at school. I think he must have been lying down in his car when you picked me up, but when we drove past, he popped his head up. He looked at me and smiled."

Shay's pale skin turned positively ashen. Then he sat up and ripped out his IV, the blood pressure cuff, the pulse oximeter, and everything else monitoring his vital signs. A nurse came running into the room, but before the baffled woman could say anything, he bellowed, "Get my clothes. I'm leaving right now!"

Porter jumped to his feet and kicked the checkers game. "I hate that stupid game. And I hate you!"

"You little bastard!" Freddie crawled along the floor picking up pieces. "You're just upset because you can't beat me."

"I did once!" Porter shouted, then ran up the stairs trying to reach what he hoped was an unlocked door and freedom. Before he could get to the top, Freddie caught him and pulled him back down the stairs, then boxed his ear.

While Porter cried, Freddie put the game back in its case and picked up it. "You need to learn to behave and show some gratitude for all I'm doing for you!"

"You aren't doing anything!" Porter yelled.

"No?" Freddie went up to the top of the stairs and unlocked the door. "I'm the only thing keeping you two brats alive. I'm going to get you something to eat. That'll make you feel better. Then, we're going to play checkers, and you're going to like it."

fter helping Shay and Hannah into Vito's truck for him to drive them back to Shay's house, Rebecca told Richie she was going to try to find Varg Hague.

"I'm going with you," Richie said. "I think your partner is worthless."

He followed her in his car to Hague's apartment. A doorman stopped them.

"We're here to see Varg Hague," Rebecca said showing her badge.

Seeing it, the doorman stood a bit straighter. "He's not in."

"Any idea when he might return?" Rebecca asked.

"I don't know. I haven't seen him for a couple of days."

"Precisely when did you last see him?" Rebecca asked.

The doorman thought a moment. "Two nights ago. We've got quite a security system here that tracks door openings and keys used." He pressed a few buttons on the console in front of him. "Looks like he left his apartment at 6:30 the next morning and hasn't returned since."

Rebecca and Richie glanced at each other and left. As they returned to their cars, Richie said, "In my experience, doormen know all about everyone's comings and goings—and who they come and go with. I think being nosy is a job requirement. Security systems can be overridden, but I believe him when he says he hasn't seen Hague since before Paula Forsyth was killed."

Rebecca nodded. "That could mean Hague was involved in the killing, or he's realized he's a target and, as you said, is in hiding."

When they reached the Blaxor Pharmaceuticals building, the building was completely dark—no indoor night lights, no outside lights. It looked deserted.

They walked to the entrance to see that a chain had been looped between the handles of the glass doors and held together with a padlock. Richie used the flashlight on his phone to read a sign on the door. "Business Closed. For more information, contact …" followed by a list of phone numbers.

Rebecca pulled out her phone and was about to call the first contact when it rang. She didn't recognize the caller's number. "Inspector Mayfield," she answered.

"Hello. This is Dinesh Singh from the Daylight Market. I was calling to tell you the sandwiches you ordered are all ready for pickup."

She was momentarily perplexed, and then everything made sense. "Yes, Mr. Singh. I understand. He's in your store now?"

"Yes."

"I'll get there as soon as I can. You might try to keep an eye on him to see which way he goes, but do not follow him. He's dangerous."

"All right," the grocer's voice sounded upbeat, as if speaking to a customer. She guessed the suspect was nearby. "See you soon."

"Thanks. Be careful."

She faced Richie. "I've got to go. The kidnapping suspect, the man who shot Shay, is in a grocery store. I'm heading over there now. Would you work on those phone numbers," she gestured toward the list on the door. "See what you can find out about Hague."

"You can't go after him alone," Richie said, grabbing her arms. "I'm coming."

"No. No way! I'll call for back-up. I've got to run."

"Which grocery store," he yelled as she ran to her SUV.

"Daylight Market, in Bayshore," she replied as she started the engine and raced off.

As she dodged traffic, she called Jared, explained the situation, and asked him to meet her. "First call the SVU and let Cheryl Wong know what's happening, then ask Eastwood to get backup ready. If we see the suspect, it might take more than the two of us to bring him in."

"Will do," he said. "See you soon."

Jared punched a number already recorded on his phone. "This is Jared," he said when no one answered and he got a voice mail recording. "Call me. It's urgent."

He put the phone down and waited. Less than a minute passed before it rang.

"Why are you phoning me?" He recognized Commissioner Barcelli's voice.

"Normally, I would have called Ms. Cahill, but …" Jared shrugged, then waited.

"Yes, yes. What's going on?"

"Mayfield has a lead on the kidnapper of Daryl Hawley's children. She's asking for my help, plus SVU's and some backup."

"Kidnapper? What do I care about a kidnapper?" Barcelli snapped.

"All I know is he seems to be connected to Blaxor. Why or how, I have no idea."

"Damn," Barcelli muttered. "Who does Mayfield think she is, ordering the whole police department around at her beck and call? She expects people to be pulled off their assigned duties to go after some lead she thinks she *may* have on someone who *may* be a kidnapper? Ridiculous. She's blown up an unimportant situation in her own mind to seem bigger than it really is."

As Jared listened to this rant, he couldn't put Barcelli's opinion of Rebecca together with the woman he'd worked with the past few days.

"And doesn't she realize," Barcelli continued, "that I'm doing all I can to hold back the public from crucifying the entire police department for not being able to protect the city's deputy mayor! She's crazy."

Jared hated talking to Barcelli. He'd pretty much despised the man for the past eight years, even as he watched him slither up through the ranks with all the ease of an eel in muddy water. "She's going after a potential kidnapper." He tried to sound calm and reasonable. "We don't know if he's armed, but we should expect he is. It's a dangerous situation."

Barcelli breathed so heavily into the phone he reminding Jared of a bull snorting before it stampeded. "Maybe. Maybe not," Barcelli said. "You know she's a hothead and will go off on any tangent that strikes her. She's done it plenty of times in the past. Be careful that you don't end up risking your life because of her shenanigans."

"No, but—"

Barcelli's voice grew louder. "She leaps to conclusions, uses her so-called 'women's intuition' as if men in the department aren't nearly as good because we lack an intuitive gene, or what-ever the hell women are supposed to have."

"I know, but—"

"I think it's a bad idea to divert resources based on Mayfield's say so. She's a lone wolf. It's best to wait and see what does or doesn't develop. It could be another wild goose chase of hers. Of course, I suggest you keep this between us. Don't even tell your boss that you've phoned me. This is all need-to-know stuff, and Eastwood doesn't need to know right now."

"Right," he murmured.

"So I guess you'd better give both the SVU and Eastwood a heads-up call. Don't leave Mayfield out in the cold. But feel free to hint that you don't find the situation as dangerous as Mayfield does. It's only a hunch of hers, and a weak one at that. Now, if this suspected kidnapper is for real and actually does get violent and starts shooting at her, well, take care of yourself. It's one thing if she does happen to put herself at risk on a mere suspicion, but I won't have her take another cop down with her. Understand?"

A shudder rippled down Jared's back. "Yes, sir." He had gotten the message.

34

A s soon as Richie watched Rebecca drive away, a bad feeling struck. She was relying on her new partner to help. Richie didn't like it one little bit.

He took out his phone to call the first number posted on the Blaxor Pharmaceutical building, but stopped. "Screw this," he muttered. He took a photo of the phone numbers. He'd deal with them later, after he knew Rebecca was safe.

When there was trouble—and he felt certain Rebecca was heading into trouble—he always relied on Shay, Vito, and himself. But Shay needed time to recover, and his mind was wrapped around Hannah, probably simultaneously furious and scared half out of his wits that Hannah could have been the target of a kidnapper. And Vito was staying with them, keeping an eye not only on Hannah until the kidnapper was caught, but also on Shay.

And then Richie thought of the perfect person to help. He made a phone call.

"It's Richie Amalfi," he said at the sound of Sutter's voice. "Rebecca needs your help. Do you still have a badge and a gun?"

Sutter hesitated a moment. "Well, yes. I haven't signed any

paperwork yet. What's going on? Is it the Hawley case with the missing kids?"

"That, and more," Richie said. "People are dying all around her. And I'm afraid she might be next."

"What!"

"She's heading for the Daylight Market in the Bayshore."

"I know the place. I can be there in twenty minutes."

"Make it fifteen."

Rebecca hurried into the Daylight Market. Dinesh Singh told her the man had already left. He'd tried to converse, to slow him down, but reached a point where he couldn't stall any longer.

He pointed out the direction the man had gone. He'd trailed him a little way until the guy turned around as if he sensed he was being followed. Singh hurried back to his store, but he thought the man might have turned down Balou.

Rebecca got in her car, sent a text to Jared saying where to meet her, and drove to the area Singh had indicated.

She saw the abandoned mortuary, an empty commercial building, and an apartment complex that had been government-built housing. The apartments had been cheaply constructed to begin with and became so run down it was more cost effective to tear them down and start over than to renovate. Unfortunately, no private business was interested in putting money into the derelict area, and the city had been stymied as it faced nothing but protests over making any change that could affect the environment.

The apartment complex was the most likely location, yet the mortuary most intrigued her. It kept coming up for some reason. Jared had supposedly checked out this block, including the mortuary, when looking for the kids. He had reported that the city had taken possession of it after the owner abandoned it. He also said the place was locked up and empty.

As Rebecca looked around, the thought struck, what if uniform the kidnapper wore was that of a security guard? A few buildings around here had them, particularly at night. If so, he might have master keys to some of the buildings, or access to some very good lock picks or bump keys.

As she drove by the front of the mortuary, it seemed quite dead which, she guessed, was only appropriate. She parked at the end of the block. If anyone was inside, she didn't want to let it be known she was approaching.

She sat in her car and waited for Jared, wondering where he was. Earlier, she'd texted him, told him to meet her here. He hadn't replied.

This time she phoned, but he didn't answer. What the hell? Was he already falling into Bill Sutter's mode, where she would be left to tackle things alone, and he would arrive for the clean-up. Although, she had to admit, Sutter always came immediately when the situation seemed at all dangerous. And the potential was high that this one was.

Exasperated, she grew tired of waiting. She could at least check the grounds of the mortuary. If anyone was living inside, she might spot some sign of it.

Finally, she left her car and crept down the street. As expected, the front doors of the mortuary were locked.

She paused, again looking for Jared, then continued around the side of the building. There, she saw a doorway. She hurried past it to the parking area in the back. It looked neglected.

She returned to the door. Locked. Next to it was a window. Also locked.

She knew all about the need to get a search warrant, etc., but she carried a lock pick and the door was simply too tempting to pass up.

Maybe it was good Jared wasn't with her after all.

She texted Jared to let him know she was going inside the mortuary and then shut off the sound on her phone.

She picked the lock and quietly opened the door, then took out her gun and penlight. She was tempted to see if the lights worked, but decided not to in case someone was hiding inside.

Staying close to the walls, she cautiously proceeded down the hall. She didn't know if it was because the building had been a mortuary or some other reason, but she felt her skin prickle. It was almost as if she wasn't alone, as if someone might be watching … listening.

She checked in the men's and women's rooms and saw that there was water in the toilet bowls. She guessed that, as usual, the city hadn't bothered to turn off the utilities.

She made her way to the main viewing room. It was large and empty. She suspected if people had been living here, this was where they would have settled.

She checked two tiny viewing rooms, which were even less interesting than the first.

Finally, she tucked her gun into the holster at her back. The mortuary appeared empty. Searching any further seemed to be a waste of time.

35

P orter clutched the red checker he'd just captured. His whole body stiffened and his eyes met Molly's. It seemed as if she'd stopped breathing as they listened to what sounded like footsteps on the floor above.

Freddie was silent and motionless, although he looked as if he was ready to spring at any moment. "Keep your mouths shut!" His voice was hushed but harsh. "One peep out of you and I'll hurt you."

Molly grasped her brother's hand. Hers was cold. He was sure his was, too. He figured she was praying as hard as he was right now for those footsteps to belong to someone who'd come to rescue them.

Freddie stood as silently as possible, walked to the light switch, flicked it quickly, and darkness again swept over the room.

Porter wanted so much to scream. To yell out. But Freddie scared him, he'd made him fear for his life and Molly's. The man was crazy. He just might kill them both if they made a sound.

The footsteps stopped, they started again, then stopped once more. Had the person found the door? Would he or she open it, come down the stairs and find them? He hoped.

And then the steps moved away again. Farther and farther. Until they disappeared altogether.

Minutes went by. Long minutes, when all he heard was his breathing and the beat of his heart.

Then Freddie flipped the lights back on.

He had a huge grin on his face. "Now, let's get back to our game of checkers."

36

Richie nearly wore a groove in the sidewalk as he waited for Sutter to arrive. As soon as he saw Rebecca's former partner, he ran into the street. Sutter stopped, and Richie jumped into the passenger seat. "She's not here. The grocer said she's probably on Balou Street."

"Tell me what's happening," Sutter said as he spun into a U-turn and headed toward Balou.

"Rebecca has a lead on the kidnapper of the Hawley kids," Richie said. "The grocer spotted him. She doesn't know who he is, but the grocer gave a description."

"Good."

"Rebecca expects her new partner to give her back-up—Jared Woolridge. But I don't trust him."

Sutter thin lips tightened. "I've heard about the guy. I don't blame you."

Rebecca was walking toward the door to leave the mortuary when she stopped. There was something odd about the place, something that bothered her—something other than the creepiness inside. It was almost as if the place was holding its breath. As if it weren't as empty as she assumed.

She turned back, some sixth sense telling her that she'd missed something, that she needed to give it a more thorough search.

This time she stepped slowly, carefully, as soundlessly as she could. If someone was inside, she didn't want to send up alarms as she might have done earlier.

She returned to what had been the mortuary's main viewing room and studied it from one end to the other. Thick drapes hung along the nearby walls and over windows. Nothing out of the ordinary there. But she decided to make sure nothing lurked behind.

She could scarcely believe it: behind one drape was a door.

She told herself it probably was nothing, perhaps a small closet.

She quietly opened the door to find a full room. She guessed it might have once been an office or a room where supplies and extra furniture had been kept when the mortuary was functioning. At the far side of the room she saw another door.

She crossed the room, tried it and found it locked. Why, she wondered, was this door was locked when others inside the mortuary hadn't been.

The possibility of the building having a large basement crossed her mind, but they weren't common in San Francisco, and rarely found in poor areas like this one. It had to do with the cost, the high water table, and the fact that lots of the land near the bay was fill which made it unstable. Plus, many people still had the old fear that in an earthquake a house could fall into the big hole a basement created.

It would have made sense that this door led to a closet, but a hint of light from the other side peeked out from the threshold. Something was behind the door. She had to find out what.

She was taking out her lock pick when she heard what she thought were voices. She put her ear against the door.

"King me." It was a man's voice.

"You cheated." That voice wasn't a man's. It was a child's.

Her heart pounded. The kidnapped children?

They hadn't heard her—at least not this time.

She put her pick in the lock, trying not to make a sound, but even to her ears the click of the pick was too loud for comfort. The voices stopped, except for the faint sound of someone saying "Keep quiet."

But it wasn't quiet she heard now, it was a voice—a high-pitched child's voice.

"We're down here!"

Down? She'd been right about the basement.

She hit the door with her shoulder, but it wouldn't budge.

Then another voice, louder.

"Help us!"

Then a scream.

She had no time to fiddle with lock picks. She fired at the lock and shattered it, then kicked open the door and crouched beside the doorframe.

Gun drawn, she tried to see what was past the door, but the light she'd seen through the threshold was gone now. She saw only blackness.

She heard footsteps, but could see nothing.

Was it the man coming toward her? Or one of the children?

"You can turn on the light if you want," the man said, his voice calm but vile. "The switch is at the top of the stairs, just to your left. But if you do turn it on, if you see me, there's no telling what I'll do to these children."

She pulled back, trying to decide what to do.

"Leave me alone!" a boy shouted.

In the dark, Rebecca heard scuffling, stumbling. Falling.

"Porter!" a girl cried.

Rebecca switched on the light.

37

R ichie and Sutter walked along Balou Street looking for Rebecca or any sign of where she might be. Richie had tried phoning her, but she didn't answer. Sutter had no better luck.

"There!" Richie pointed at her car parked up ahead. "She's got to be nearby. But where?"

Sutter suddenly grabbed Richie and pulled him back against a building where they were less visible. "Someone's sitting in the mid-sized sedan across the street, three cars down."

Richie looked at the car Sutter indicated. The glow of a street lamp let him just barely make out the person inside. "I can't be sure, but that could be her new partner. If so, why the hell is he just sitting there?"

"Good question," Sutter said with a sneer. "I'm told he's a brown noser of the worst sort. He'd turn in his mother if it meant being praised by higher ups."

"Yeah, well, something tells me he got the detail only because someone high up pulled strings. Like maybe the police commissioner himself."

"Since I'm supposed to be enjoying retirement," Sutter could barely hide his contempt for the idea, "why don't you talk to him while I look around. Maybe there's a good reason he's sitting around looking like the piece of shit that he is."

Richie was surprised at Sutter. He'd never seen or heard the guy so vehement. "Okay," he said and hurried to Jared.

He tapped on the window.

Jared jumped and spun around, gun in hand. He lowered it when he saw Richie and then rolled down the window. "What are you doing here?"

"Where's Rebecca?"

"I don't know. I'm waiting for her."

Richie didn't believe him. "Didn't you see her car parked at the corner?"

"No. But if it's there, she must be near. She's probably checking out one of these buildings." Jared eyed Richie. "You shouldn't be here. You're no cop."

"What say we try to find her?" Richie suggested.

"How do we do that?" Jared wrinkled his mouth. "Look at these empty buildings. She could be in any one of them. If we choose wrong, we'll miss her. That's why I'm waiting for her to send me a text."

"So we wait?" Richie asked.

"That's the smart thing to do."

Richie didn't like it. He also didn't see Bill Sutter anywhere. He wondered if Jared had noticed the man whose place he'd taken.

"You can wait," he told Jared. "I'm not."

"A lot of cops should be showing up here fairly soon. Don't blame me if you get shot accidentally," Jared said. "Consider this a warning."

∼

Relieved that the Hawley children were still alive, Rebecca knew it was up to her to keep them that way.

The man the grocer had identified was holding the terrified little girl tight against his body, a knife at her neck. She looked so darn small, so thin and frightened, Rebecca could scarcely breathe from fear of making the wrong move, saying the wrong word, and causing the monster holding her to end the child's life.

Porter lay sprawled on the floor and was just starting to sit up. He was dazed and winced in pain. Rebecca suspected the kidnapper had shoved him there. Violently.

The children's faces and hands were caked with tear-streaked soot and dirt. Their clothes were torn and grimy. Filthy blankets lay on the cement floor along with empty food and drink containers.

Rebecca stared at the man. He was exactly as the grocer had described. Portly, not too tall, early-to-mid thirties, with shaggy brown hair. His clothes were loose fitting, and his shoulders rounded and stooped as if the extra weight he carried pulled him down.

Yet, seeing him in the flesh, Rebecca felt there was something vaguely familiar about him. She didn't recognize his face ... but something else niggled at her ...

"Let the girl go," Rebecca said. "Please, she's just a child."

"I know. She's my child now." His grip on Molly tightened. "I don't want to hurt her, but you're here to take her away from me. I won't let you do that. She needs me. They both need me."

"Relax, please," Rebecca said, trying to sound calm and soothing. "I understand. I won't take her away. But remove the knife. It's too close. She might get scared, try to run, and end up badly hurt. You don't want that."

He lifted the knife from Molly's neck, but still held it much too close to the child's face and eyes.

"Can Porter come to me?" Rebecca said as she slowly descended the steps. "He won't do anything to you."

He watched Rebecca in stone faced silence.

She reached the bottom and held out her arms. Porter took a quick glance at the man and then ran into Rebecca's arms. He was shaking as he held onto her.

"Porter!" Molly started to cry.

"Shut up!" the man jostled her, which only made her cry louder. "If you don't want this at your neck again, *shut up!*" He put the knife in front of her face.

"Don't cry, Molly," Rebecca said. Porter's arms were tight around her waist, his face buried against her. "We won't leave you. It'll be okay."

"Put your gun on the ground," the man ordered. "And kick it over to me."

She had Porter move off to her side, then lowered her Beretta and flung it, but not too hard, in the kidnapper's direction. "Who are you?"

"Nobody."

"You've taken care of these kids. How did you know to do that?" she asked.

"What do you mean?"

"How did you get them to come here? Away from their home, their parents?"

"Their father's dead," the man announced.

Porter nodded, looking so sad and distraught that Rebecca drew him to her side again, keeping him close, as she backed away from the man and Molly. She realized Porter and Molly already knew of their father's death.

She eyed the kidnapper. "How do you know he's dead?"

"Maybe it was a good guess," he said with a smile.

"You killed him," she stated, taking a couple more steps backward, trying to get closer to the wall at the bottom of the stairs.

His eyebrows lifted, and a smirk filled his face.

She paused, needing to proceed without being too confrontational. "How did you know about this place, that it had water and electricity?"

"I'm a smart guy. And you aren't nearly as clever as you think. Now, you know too much. And it's going to cost you." He gestured at Porter. "Boy, open up that coffin."

Porter saw where the man pointed. He shook his head.

"Open it now, or I'll hurt Molly!"

Porter looked frozen in fear.

"Did you hear me, boy? Or don't you care about your sister?"

Rebecca gently nudged Porter. He glanced up, and she nodded. He slowly walked over to the casket, glancing back and forth between Rebecca and their captor. It was a struggle for the boy to lift the lid, but he finally managed to.

"Now, Miss Cop, get inside."

When the kidnapper had used the word "sister," something jarred Rebecca's memory. Maybe it was the almost reverent way he said it, maybe because, although she had only seen him in the courtroom once, he had spent the day hiding his face in his arms, his thick, rounded shoulders rocking slightly as he whimpered, "She was my sister, my sister," over and over.

"I know you," Rebecca whispered, staring at him. "You're Sharon Lynch's brother. Your name ...?"

"Frederick. Frederick Lynch, and soon nobody will forget it ever again!" He said all that proudly, but then his face turned bitter, ugly. "You let her killer go free. None of you cared about my sister. She did nothing but try to do good in this life. To help homeless people, children who ran away from their bad homes— much like these two did. And when she was killed, you only pretended to care. You let her murderer go. Not enough evidence, they said. It was *your fault!* If you had done your job right,

Virginia Kirk would be on death row now. Instead, she's walking around free."

Rebecca could scarcely believe what she was hearing. She remembered that Sharon Lynch and Daryl Hawley had worked together and inadvertently had uncovered a crooked scheme about Lulz ... and her thoughts raced to those who had profited from the scheme ...

My God, she thought, this is a brother's mad revenge.

"All these murders are about Sharon Lynch?"

"You sound surprised, as if she isn't worth anything. She was my sister! I have no one else now. No one. But all of you will pay for her murder: Daryl Hawley and his fat wife, the bastards at Blaxor, Dianne Cahill, Clive Hutchinson, and Virginia Kirk. All of them. Now I can add you and your worthless partner! All of you will pay for her death, and my grief."

38

Shay waited until Vito fell asleep, then he loaded his Sig Sauer and headed for the mortuary on Balou Street. He realized he had driven directly to Hannah's school from the mortuary the two times she had seen the scumbag.

It had to be where the kidnapper was hiding.

Shay could have kicked himself. In the past, he would have picked up in an instant that someone was following him. Now, he had too much on his mind. His thoughts were all about Hannah and her mother. He remembered how he had been thinking about Salma Najjar's car and wondering if it was still parked out by Ocean Beach collecting parking tickets. He had been far too busy recently to check on it.

Then he had pondered Hannah's situation at school and how he should handle that.

Not paying enough attention had nearly done him in.

Now, before heading to the mortuary, he opened the app that tracked the GPS on Richie's phone. He had installed it so that if Richie was in trouble—and considering some of the people he dealt with, it was a distinct possibility—Shay would have some idea of where to find him.

He figured Richie and Rebecca were together and looking for the kidnapper, and he wanted to see where they were at the moment.

The tracker showed Richie in the Bayview-Hunters Point area, which confirmed to Shay that his instincts to go to the mortuary were right.

He only hoped he'd be able to find the pervert before either Richie or Rebecca did. Because if he did, he'd make sure there was nothing left for Rebecca to arrest.

"Get inside the damned coffin!" Frederick Lynch roared. The way he was yelling and shaking caused the knife to prick Molly. She cried out and a drop of blood appeared on her neck. Her brother trembled as he watched.

Rebecca's breath caught. Freddie moved the knife slightly, but the menace remained clear.

"I said," he yelled at Rebecca. "Move it!"

She had always heard coffins were airtight to keep down the body's putrefaction as long as possible. It was the last place she wanted to go. Suffocation was a slow, horrific death. Still, the danger to Molly forced her to take a step toward the coffin.

"I'm not getting inside that thing without some answers." Rebecca stopped, keeping eye contact with the man. "The least you can do is tell me why you killed Daryl Hawley. He was just a driver. Apparently he liked Sharon. And he never hurt anyone."

"That's what you think!"

"Who did he hurt?"

"He betrayed my sister! When the two of them figured out the city was buying a lot more drugs from Blaxor than were delivered, Sharon planned to let the world know. Dianne Cahill and everyone working with her would have gone to jail. My sister would have been a hero! Instead, Hawley told his wife, a Blaxor employee, who blabbed to the boss. Daryl Hawley betrayed her. He got her killed."

"But why take the kids?"

His eyes hardened. "Because they'll be orphans soon. I knew Hawley had kids. I also knew he had a rotten wife—the bitch who tattled to her Blaxor bosses. I was going to kill her quickly, but when I saw how much she was suffering, I decided to wait. I want her to know how it feels to lose someone you love. Not her worthless husband, but her kids. She can suffer their loss the way I suffered when Sharon was killed."

"But still, why do you want them?" Rebecca pressed.

"Why not? With both parents dead, I know what kind of terrible life they'll have. My sister and I were in the system. Foster homes. All that crap. We were once happy, just like those two. Then it all turned bad. I have no one now. And soon they'll have no one. Why shouldn't we have each other?"

"That's quite nice," Rebecca said. "A real plan."

He laughed. "Isn't it? And you don't fool me. I don't care what you think of me. Now get inside, I said!"

"I agree with you, but I still don't get it." She stepped backward again, shaking her head.

His curiosity seemed to get the better of him. "You agree?"

"Virginia Kirk. She killed your sister. I absolutely agree with you there. But you've let her live. Why?"

He snorted. "She's in hiding, not even in the state. But I won't give up. Eventually, I *will* find her. And she *will* die."

"Dianne Cahill." Rebecca tossed out the name quickly. "She's got security. How did you reach her?"

He smiled eerily. "She drank too much, that's how. I sent her a text saying I was a 'concerned citizen.' I said Clive Hutchinson had been in an auto accident. The EMTs were working on him, but it looked like he wouldn't make it. He was asking for her. If she hurried ... and she did." He chuckled. "You should have seen her face. 'Where is he? Where is he?' she kept asking, and then, *bam!*"

"God." Rebecca could only imagine the horror that went through Cahill's mind. She almost felt sorry for her.

"Now," his hand tightened around the knife, "get the hell inside that casket, or I'll shoot you with your own gun and dump you in there myself."

"Take it easy," Rebecca said. "I'm going." The wall, the light switch, was almost at arm's length. She had to be fast and accurate if she made a leap for it. She looked at where her gun lay on the ground about halfway between the two of them. She just had to make sure that, in the dark, she could keep her perspective on direction and distance. "Look, you don't want the kids to see this. Send them upstairs."

"No way."

"Then, at least send them to the back of the room."

"That makes no sense," he scoffed.

"Yes. It does. You don't want them to remember you making me get inside the coffin and shutting the lid, and then hearing me pound on the lid because you cut off my air, *killing me*. You know that sort of thing can traumatize a child for life."

"Shut up!"

"I'll do what you say, but I don't want them to be close to your knife. They might try something—who knows? You don't want them hurt and bleeding, do you?"

"All right! Maybe you do care about the kids. It makes sense!" He glanced at the children. "You two brats—she wants you across the room. Don't worry. This won't take long. She'll stop talking and we'll be able to get back to our game."

"What game is that?" Rebecca asked. She knew he would go for her gun next. She had to act before that happened.

"I said *shut up!* Too damn many questions." He glared at the kids.

Rebecca gestured for Porter to go to Molly. He took a few steps and held out his hand. The man let Molly go. She took Porter's hand and the two of them slowly walked toward the far wall.

For the first time, Rebecca allowed her eyes to travel, to leave Frederick Lynch and the children. She took a good look at the dolls in the distance and couldn't stop herself from gasping. The color of the hair, the short, blunt style—they were the same as Sharon Lynch's. And the doll's red, drawn on tears were beyond macabre.

She forced her gaze away from them and back to the killer.

As soon as she saw his attention heavy on the children, and that they were safely out of the way of gunfire, she turned and hurled herself at the light switch, hitting it to shut it off, then dropping to the ground where she'd hope the darkness would shield her as she tried to reach her gun.

But the doors at the top of the stairs had all been left open, and just enough light trickled into the gloomy basement that he could see her movements. He raced toward the gun, holding his knife outward in her direction.

She could see him as well, see the glint of the knife. She stopped herself just short of it ... and of her gun.

He chuckled as he bent over to pick up her Beretta. "Lose something?"

Just then he became illuminated in the beam of a flashlight. "Police! Drop it!" a voice yelled, and immediately after, a shot rang out.

Freddie clutched his neck as blood sprayed from it, and then he fell forward at Rebecca's feet, dead.

Rebecca stared at him, shocked. Then she spun toward the

sound of footsteps on the stairs. The flashlight blinded her from seeing who held it.

She ran to the light switch and flipped it on. Coming down the stairs, gun in one hand, flashlight in the other, was Bill Sutter.

"... or I'll shoot," Sutter said. He faced Rebecca and shrugged. "I guess us retirees do things a little more slowly than you young folk. But I did warn him."

"I heard you loud and clear," she said. "Thank you, Bill."

Richie hurried down the stairs behind Sutter, and as soon as he could get past the older man, he reached Rebecca and his strong arms circled her. "Are you all right?"

She held him tight. "Yes, we all are now, thank God."

The kids ran to her. She bent down and put her arms around them both, holding them close.

Sutter stood over the dead man. "Holy shit! I know this guy. Sharon Lynch's brother."

"You know him?" Richie asked, trying to make sense out of this latest bit of news.

"He was always bugging me, insisting I see that justice was done for Sharon." Sutter stroked his chin. "I was the public face of the investigation, always on TV, so he always ranted and raved at me. And Blaxor ... good God, was he right all along?"

"What do you mean?" Rebecca and Richie both asked.

"He had a conspiracy theory that Sharon was a would-be whistle-blower and had been killed to silence her. But it sounded too crazy. Without any proof at all, who would ever believe a story like that? Especially since, as odd as Sharon Lynch was, her brother was an obvious whack job, five cans short of a six-pack."

Rebecca gawked at him. "If you had still been on the case, the moment we had a drawing of the suspect, you'd have known who he was, and why he was involved. We need you back on the force, Bill. I need you!"

Sutter's thin face spread into a smile. "That's good to hear."

Richie turned to the kids. "How would you guys like to go home?"

The sound of "Yays" filled the old mortuary.

Bill Sutter then phoned Lt. Eastwood. "One, I'm not retiring," he announced loudly with a wink at Rebecca, "and two, send a team out to the address I'm going to give you. I just shot a murderer. Yes, to death! What do you think? And not only that, I helped rescue the missing kids."

Rebecca couldn't help but smile as she and Richie led the kids up the stairs. Just as they reached the top, a familiar shape appeared in front of them.

"He's already dead," Richie said, then patted Shay's good shoulder. "Better luck next time."

39

Rebecca stood outside the mortuary with the children, Richie beside her. Crime scene technicians, patrol officers, the medical examiner and her team, and EMTs to take the children to the hospital to be checked had all arrived. She watched as the SVU investigator who had gone to pick up Tracy Hawley returned to the scene. He no sooner stopped the car than Tracy jumped out of it, arms outstretched as she rushed to her children. Molly and Porter ran into her arms and all began to cry as they hugged each other, Tracy giving everyone her heartfelt thanks.

Rebecca felt both joy and relief watching them. As she fought back threatening tears, she told herself it had just been a long, tough week and that she was tired—not at all a sentimental sap who was touched by the happy reunion. After all it was what they'd all been hoping and working for.

"Are you okay?" Richie asked.

"Getting better. I'm always relieved when an investigation is over, but this one more than others."

He nodded, curling a lock of her hair behind her ear. She would have loved to let him put his arms around her, but that would have to come later. Too many coworkers were near, and she always tried to project herself as one tough cop around them, no matter what she was feeling inside.

Richie remained outdoors as Rebecca rejoined Bill Sutter in the mortuary's basement, making sure the crime scene technicians covered all the areas she wanted. The kids seemed to have survived remarkably well in this horrible place, but she understood that Freddie had tortured them mentally. She fully expected it would take them a while to get past the nightmares sure to come. She decided to check in on them from time to time, just to make sure they were doing all right.

Jared had turned up briefly when the crime scene technicians arrived, saying something about keeping guard outside and having had no idea any of this was happening in the darkened mortuary. Then he disappeared.

Shay had gone home, satisfied that the kidnapper was dead, but dejected that it hadn't happened at his hands. A typical Shay response.

Finally, it was well past ten p.m. when Rebecca, Richie, and Bill Sutter walked into Homicide. They were surprised to find Lieutenant Eastwood as well as three of the other inspectors, Paavo, Yosh and Calderon, waiting for them.

Eastwood led them in applause. "You not only found the kids, but solved three murders! Great going!"

"It was a good team effort," Rebecca said, with nods to both Richie and Sutter.

"Along with Rebecca's unwillingness to give up," Sutter said.

"So where's our new boy wonder?" Yosh asked in his big, boisterous voice.

"I don't know," Rebecca said.

Sutter shook his head.

"Last I saw him, he was hiding in his car," Richie said. "Probably waiting for someone to pull his strings."

"Didn't he ask you to send back-up?" Rebecca asked Eastwood.

"He said you thought you might need some if you found the kidnapper in the area, but it was unlikely you would. I was waiting to hear back from him. Still haven't, in fact," Eastwood said with a frown.

"He's probably crying on his daddy's shoulder," Calderon said. "As in 'sugar daddy.'"

"What do you mean?" Eastwood asked.

"No one will really say, but when Barcelli was his precinct captain, a prisoner died under their watch. It was covered up faster than you can say 'commissioner.' And next thing you knew Barcelli and Woolridge were both moved out of the precinct and into admin offices."

"Don't stop now," Yosh said.

"I have to." Calderon shrugged. "No one will say anything more except that they've 'heard disturbing rumors' about Barcelli. But I think they're worried about their jobs if they speak out."

"Yosh and I have already come across people afraid to talk as we try to investigate Dianne Cahill's death," Paavo said. "It looks like she was involved in big a real estate scam, but when we ask for specific evidence that ought to exist, we're told it's either lost or misplaced."

"This whole mess is like fish," Yosh added. "It stinks from the head."

"Typical," Richie said. "And of course it will all be covered up. Heaven forbid anyone allow the city's government to look less than stellar, even if one of the really bad apples is the police commissioner."

Eastwood was looking more and more uncomfortable but held his tongue.

"We have to hope," Rebecca said, "that the worst of those bad apples will soon be gone. And we can take that as a win."

Just then Jared walked into Homicide.

"Hey, good work out there, guys!" he said with a big smile.

"Woolridge," Eastwood said, stepping forward. "Into my office. We need to talk."

They all stared in silence as the two entered Eastwood's office and the door closed.

Yosh's eyebrows rose nearly to his hairline. "Shit's hittin' the fan now."

40

Vito headed for home the next day, and once out from under his watchful eye, Shay took a quick drive to Ocean Beach. With all that had happened, he hadn't been back there for a while.

He went directly to the parking area where he'd left Salma Najjar's car.

He froze, scarcely able to believe what he was seeing. A tow truck had just finished hooking up Hannah's mother's small sedan and was now driving off with it.

A month or so earlier Shay had parked the car in that spot, abandoning it with the surety some police officer or meter maid would soon find that it had overstayed the admissible parking time and called to have it towed away. But for weeks, that hadn't happened.

His thoughts went to the note he'd put in the car, and he couldn't help but think of all the changes that had taken place in his life and Hannah's since he'd written it. The note was supposedly from Salma Najjar—a suicide note that contained a confession to murder. He had expected that a towing company would find the note and turn it over to the police, to Rebecca Mayfield, and she would close her open murder investigation.

But now the holes in his plan rushed at him. What if Rebecca didn't believe the note? What if she began to investigate again? What if, somehow, she tracked down Salma?

And no matter what Rebecca did, the press would pick up the story and bring Salma's case, her confession and possible suicide, to the public's attention once more. Would it be possible for him, again, to keep such news from Hannah? Something told him he had better be prepared for her to hear about it one way or another.

He could have kicked himself for coming up with the idea of a suicide note. Back when he had only himself to think about, he thought the plan was a good one.

Now, not so much.

Much as he wracked his brain, it seemed there was no way to stop the ugly fallout that would result.

But he would try, whatever it took.

Two mornings later, Richie and Rebecca, their arms around each other's waist, stood on the street in front of his house and waved good-bye as Lorene's SUV disappeared down the hill. She was on her way back to Idaho.

"Not a moment too soon," Richie muttered.

Rebecca chuckled as her arm tightened around him. "You didn't enjoy my mother being here with us?"

"About as much as a root canal," he said. "Actually, that may be too generous."

Rebecca smiled, but she was glad that the last days of her mother's visit went relatively smoothly, and that they seemed to find a bit of a truce. It was, at least, a good start.

Richie picked up the morning *Chronicle* that had been tossed on the steps to his front door. He opened it to see yet another front-page article about "hero cop" Bill Sutter who had shot and killed the man who not only kidnapped two children, but had murdered three people, including the city's deputy mayor. "Are you sure you wouldn't like to be receiving some of the glory now going to your partner?" he asked.

"About as much as you'd enjoy Lorene spending another week with us."

"That bad, huh?"

She shook her head. "Especially since Eastwood told Sutter in no uncertain terms that he was *not* to mention anything about the Blaxor drug scheme or Dianne Cahill's involvement in it. Without that, the case has no real motive and Sutter is left stammering that Freddie Lynch "simply" went on a rampage because of his sister's murder—and that Dianne Cahill was nothing but an innocent victim. Because Lynch is dead, there'll be no trial to bring out the true story."

"Maybe it's just as well," Richie said. "The city wants to keep a lid on the corruption involved."

They slowly climbed the stairs. "That's for sure." Rebecca's voice filled with disgust. "Last I heard, Clive Hutchinson will be charged with embezzlement and money laundering, and if he takes a plea deal, it'll be kept so quiet it might not even ruin his career. The only one who can open up the entire can of worms, is Varg Hague, but last I heard he's hiding in Norway—and if he hears they're close to finding him, he'll split for a non-extradition country."

At the landing, they turned to watch the morning sunrise over the city. "True." Richie grimaced. "All I can say is, if an idiot like Cornelius Wallace can remain mayor, anything's possible."

"I can't believe he didn't realize what his very own deputy and chief of staff were up to," Rebecca said.

"That's because you've never met him. The most ludicrous part is his popularity shot up five points after he cried at Dianne Cahill's funeral!"

Rebecca shook her head at the irony of it all. "What's awful, is since Eastwood asked Internal Affairs to immediately review of all the suspicious attacks on me to see who, if anyone, in the police force was involved, the department is now in turmoil."

"I guess that means Eastwood really is innocent," Richie said. "At least Barcelli had the decency to resign after rumors that some of the people who had taken strange orders from him were willing to talk to try to save their jobs, or at least, to stay out of prison."

"Jared Woolridge is among them," Rebecca added. "But I'm pretty sure he'll be handed a pink slip before this is over."

"That leaves Myron Swain." Richie's mouth wrinkled with disgust just saying the man's name.

"You can't tell me you haven't heard," Rebecca said.

"Heard what?' Richie asked.

"His body was picked up in the ocean. Someone called that they saw a man jumping off the Golden Gate Bridge. It was apparently Swain."

"My, my," Richie said with a smirk. "I guess, somehow, word got out that he was unhinged with fear of prison and ready to rat out one and all. I suspect he got an assist off the bridge. If I knew who did it, I'd shake his hand."

Rebecca gave him a sidelong glance, but decided to let the Myron Swain subject drop. "What a mess this has all been," she said. "Bizarre, dirty, and nasty."

"Not to mention deadly," Richie added, but then he turned to look directly at her, his expression serious. "Let me be sure of one thing. Your mother had a lot to say about your childhood, the family's farm, the past, the good times you had, and much how you loved it. You aren't sorry you're not going back with her, right?"

She grinned. "Do you really see me as a masochist?"

He placed his hands on her waist. "But she'd feed you

Hawaiian pizzas."

"I'll pass," she said with a shake of the head.

"What about Ed Lockhart? The way your mother talked about him, he's more than perfect for you. Your first love, your fiancé, and now he's come to his senses and is pining away."

Lips pursed, she shook her head. "Somehow, I can't imagine Ed running through an abandoned mortuary, unarmed, but ready to take on a man with a gun and a knife to save me. Ed had his chance. He lost. Thank God!"

"That's what I thought," he said smugly.

She raised an eyebrow. "On the other hand, it's nice to know if things don't work out here in the city, there's someone out there waiting for me."

He looked even more self-satisfied as he pushed open the door to his house, his head high. "You would be so bored.

She couldn't help but smile. "I'm afraid you're absolutely right."

With that, they called Spike and the three of them walked into the house. As Rebecca turned to shut the door, a feeling of relief washed over her.

In her job, she would always face danger. It came with the territory. But she should no longer need to worry that someone at work might be targeting her. She hadn't fully realized how tense and uptight the situation had made her, or how long she had carried the burden of it.

Now, in this house, temporarily at least, she could shut away the outside world, shut away danger, the past, her mother's disapproval, even the disappointments of her youthful love life, and instead be thankful for all she had—particularly for the unwavering love, support, and yes, even the excitement, that Richie offered.

The door clicked shut, and she joined Richie as a new day began.

ABOUT THE AUTHOR

Joanne Pence was born and raised in northern California. She has been an award-winning, *USA Today* best-selling author of mysteries for many years, but she has also written historical fiction, contemporary romance, romantic suspense, a fantasy, and supernatural suspense. All of her books are now available as ebooks and in print, and many are also offered in special large print editions. Joanne hopes you'll enjoy her books, which present a variety of times, places, and reading experiences, from mysterious to thrilling, emotional to lightly humorous, as well as powerful tales of times long past.

Visit her at www.joannepence.com and be sure to sign up for Joanne's mailing list to hear about new books.

The Rebecca Mayfield Mysteries

Rebecca is a by-the-book detective, who walks the straight and narrow in her work, and in her life. Richie, on the other hand, is not at all by-the-book. But opposites can and do attract, and there are few mystery twosomes quite as opposite as Rebecca and Richie.

ONE O'CLOCK HUSTLE – North American Book Award winner in Mystery

TWO O'CLOCK HEIST

THREE O'CLOCK SÉANCE

FOUR O'CLOCK SIZZLE

FIVE O'CLOCK TWIST

SIX O'CLOCK SILENCE

SEVEN O'CLOCK TARGET

Plus a Christmas Novella: The Thirteenth Santa

The Angie & Friends Food & Spirits Mysteries

Angie Amalfi and Homicide Inspector Paavo Smith are soon to be married in this latest mystery series. Crime and calories plus a new "twist" in Angie's life in the form of a ghostly family inhabiting the house she and Paavo buy, create a mystery series with a "spirited" sense of fun and adventure.

COOKING SPIRITS
ADD A PINCH OF MURDER
COOK'S BIG DAY
Plus a Christmas mystery-fantasy: COOK'S CURIOUS CHRISTMAS
And a cookbook: COOK'S DESSERT COOKBOOK

The early "Angie Amalfi mystery series" began when Angie first met San Francisco Homicide Inspector Paavo Smith. Here are those mysteries in the order written:

SOMETHING'S COOKING
TOO MANY COOKS
COOKING UP TROUBLE
COOKING MOST DEADLY
COOK'S NIGHT OUT
COOKS OVERBOARD
A COOK IN TIME
TO CATCH A COOK
BELL, COOK, AND CANDLE
IF COOKS COULD KILL
TWO COOKS A-KILLING
COURTING DISASTER
RED HOT MURDER
THE DA VINCI COOK

Supernatural Suspense
Ancient Echoes
Top Idaho Fiction Book Award Winner
Over two hundred years ago, a covert expedition shadowing Lewis and Clark disappeared in the wilderness of Central Idaho.

Now, seven anthropology students and their professor vanish in the same area. The key to finding them lies in an ancient secret, one that men throughout history have sought to unveil.

Ancient Shadows

Archeologist Michael Rempart finds himself pitted against ancient demons and modern conspirators when a dying priest gives him a powerful artifact—a pearl said to have granted Genghis Khan the power, eight centuries ago, to lead his Mongol warriors across the steppes to the gates of Vienna.

Ancient Illusions

A long-lost diary, a rare book of ghost stories, and unrelenting nightmares combine to send archeologist Michael Rempart on a forbidden journey into the occult and his own past.

Historical, Contemporary & Fantasy Romance
Dance with a Gunfighter

Gabriella Devere wants vengeance after witnessing her family's murder by a gang of outlaws. Jess McLowry, a hired gun, knows a young woman like her will have no chance against the outlaws, and vows to save her. But the price of vengeance is high and Gabriella's willingness to sacrifice everything ultimately leads to the book's deadly and startling conclusion.

Willa Cather Literary Award finalist for Best Historical Novel.

The Dragon's Lady

Turn-of-the-century San Francisco comes to life in this romance of star-crossed lovers whose love is forbidden by both society and the laws of the time. The two are from completely different worlds, and when both worlds are shattered by the Great Earthquake and Fire of 1906 that destroyed most of San Francisco, they face their ultimate test.

Seems Like Old Times

When Lee Reynolds, nationally known television news anchor, returns to the small town where she was born, little does she expect to find that her first love has moved back to town. Tony Santos had been a major league baseball player, but now finds his days of glory gone. He's gone back home to raise his young son as a single dad.

Both have changed a lot, and being together makes it seems like old times. But is it?

The Ghost of Squire House

A compelling, prickly ghost with a tortured, guilt-ridden past, and a lonely heroine determined to start fresh, find themselves in a battle of wills and emotion in this ghostly fantasy of love, time, and chance.

Dangerous Journey

With a touch of the romantic adventure film Romancing the Stone, C.J. Perkins, who is trying to find her brother, and bounty hunter Darius Kane follow a trail that takes them through the narrow streets of Hong Kong, the backrooms of San Francisco's Chinatown, and the wild jungles of Borneo. Soon, C.J. finds herself not only in danger of losing her life, but also of losing her heart.

An Astrologer's Guide to Finding Mr. Perfect

Miranda Moon decides to use her horoscope to help her find a soul mate, someone charming and debonair--someone who'll be perfect for her. At the same time, rancher Cody McCord has given up on ever finding a woman who'll want to share his hard life running a small cattle ranch. When circumstances throw them together, the result is star-crossed fun.